ARTEMIS

ROMANCING A GOD SERIES

CHARLEY MARSH

TIMBERDOODLE PRESS

INTRODUCTION

Artemis was the daughter of Zeus and Leto and virginal twin sister of Apollo. She was the goddess of the hunt, the moon, and chastity. She watched over the forests, mountains, and all wilderness, and especially the young.

Artemis was a very popular goddess and there are many conflicting tales about her. All agree however that Orion was her favorite companion. As one story goes, Artemis's twin Apollo tricked her into killing Orion when she was about to sacrifice her virginity to the man she loved.

In my humble opinion that was a lousy thing for her brother to do and I cannot let their love story end there.

CHAPTER 1

TIA SMITH STRODE through the double etched-glass doors of
Orion Development and scowled. Her first visit to the company
her father had insisted she work with on the bayside project and
she already hated them. In her opinion, a company who paid to
have the constellation Orion etched into dark smoked glass along
with their name in fancy script was a company who overcharged
their clients.

Tia was fiercely protective of the people affected by her
projects, and Bayside Commons was the largest project her
young company had put together to date. The scope of the
project would provide lots of opportunity for unscrupulous firms
to pad costs and skim off the extra.

She was determined not to let that happen with Bayside.
She'd worked too hard setting the project up to let some arrogant
businessman scupper it for her.

She paused just inside the glass doors and eyed the large,
luxurious reception area. A half dozen brown leather club chairs
ranged in cozy seating groups against one wood paneled wall to
her right. Real wood paneling, she noted. Not that fake veneer
crap that was all the rage in the last century.

The chairs were fronted by several glass coffee tables and faced a wall of windows looking out over Portland's harbor and working waterfront.

She smelled coffee, rich leather, and the faint briny smell of sea water that told her Orion Development believed in open windows.

Oil and watercolor paintings of Portland's early days hung on the paneled walls. A quick glance at the one closest to her told Tia they were originals by some of the city's finest artists.

The room looked like it belonged in a high class private men's club, not an office complex. It was an in your face reminder that Orion Development was so successful they could afford to waste a windowed wall, usually reserved for high-powered executives, on their waiting room, and consequently on their clients.

It was brilliant marketing.

Tia's scowled deepened. She despised ostentatiousness in any form. In her mind, Jack Orion's company displayed it in spades. She expected the man himself to be even worse. Damn her father and his meddling.

A little research into the highly public Orion had turned up a man who played hard and went through beautiful women like they were a bottomless commodity. In his life they probably were, she thought with disgust. Orion had everything shallow, status seeking babes wanted–money, prestige and power, and looks.

She headed across the lush deep blue carpet to the only person in the room. A receptionist sat erect behind a sleek desk built from polished mahogany that held a state of the art communication system and computer. A small name plaque identified her as Ashley Hayes.

Ms. Hayes matched the room–deep blue skirt suit, red-brown hair pulled back into a snug bun, everything neat and prim and well put together, make-up expertly applied to her slightly slanted eyes and generous lips.

In contrast, Tia was dressed to visit the building site in slim jeans, a faded Rolling Stones tee-shirt, and scuffed leather boots.

The receptionist stopped tapping the keyboard with her long nails and the faint clatter that Tia had detected upon entering the Orion offices stopped.

Much to her mother's dismay, Tia kept her own nails neatly trimmed. She couldn't stand that tap-tap-tap that long nails made when working a keyboard, something she spent many hours at. That, plus the fact that Tia worked with her hands and often beat them up, meant short nails, no polish.

"Darling, how do you expect to attract a man when you don't make the most of your feminine qualities?" Her mother's voice echoed in Tia's head.

How many times had Tia listened to her mother's lectures on luring a man?

What her poor, well-meaning mother didn't understand was that Tia had her work. The job kept her busy, usually seven days a week. So far she hadn't met any men who were more interesting than her job.

The receptionist smiled with her deep red lips–lips that exactly matched her nails–a smile that did not reach her dark brown eyes. Tia wondered if the woman always coordinated her lips and nails. Why would a person do that? Didn't the woman have better things to do with her time?

"Welcome to Orion Development. How may I help you?"

The woman's voice was smooth and cool. Obviously she didn't understand the meaning of the word "welcome" as there was none in her tone.

"Tia Smith. I have an appointment with Jack Orion," Tia answered.

The receptionist clicked a few keys. "I see you are scheduled to meet with Mr. Orion at ten o'clock."

"I just said that, didn't I? Let him know I'm here, please."

The receptionist's eyes grew even frostier. She turned away from Tia and tapped her headset. She spoke softly into it, then turned back to Tia.

"Mr. Orion will see you now," she said curtly as she rose from her desk. Even in sky high heels she barely came to Tia's shoulder. Wordlessly she walked to the back wall and opened a cleverly camouflaged door. She stepped into the office ahead of Tia.

Jack Orion's office had polished oak floors mostly covered by a large, blue Persian rug. The rug was old, the blue color far rarer than the more common red rugs. Tia's practiced eye could see that it had been well made, likely with several hundred knots per inch.

Floor to ceiling windows filled the wall to Tia's left with a leather sofa and two facing leather chairs attractively arranged in front of it. Shelves filled with books and models of buildings and ships lined the opposite wall. She had to admit that she liked the room, despite the fact that she was prepared not to like the room's occupant.

Tia's gaze rested on Jack Orion, seated behind a modern, black, U-shaped console holding three computers. He had yet to look up from the screen he was watching. "I'll be with you in a sec."

His voice was deep and smooth and softer than Tia had expected. She wondered if he sang. He had a great voice for it.

"Mr. Orion, Ms. Smith to see you." The receptionist hesitated, stepped closer to the desk. Her voice softened. "Can I get you anything, Jack? Coffee?" she asked.

"Not at the moment, Ashley. I'll let you know."

Tia watched them with detached curiosity. She found that observing the dynamics between people proved useful in her business dealings. The way a boss treated an employee told her a lot about the boss. Was he courteous? Patient? Or rude and demanding? Was the employee respectful? Over-familiar? Cowed?

It was obvious to Tia that the receptionist was definitely sweet on Jack Orion, but he had barely looked at her. He either didn't want to show any hint of romance in front of a stranger or he wasn't interested in Ashley.

The receptionist gave Tia another cold look and left the office, leaving the door open, most likely so she could eavesdrop on Tia's meeting with her boss.

Tia stepped over and closed the office door firmly behind Ashley, then moved to stand in front of the desk. This was a private meeting. She had a few things to set straight with Jack Orion and she didn't want any interruptions.

The man in question rose from his desk as she crossed the room. He was tall, at least six-five, with broad shoulders that filled out his perfectly-fitted suit, a handsome face framed by dark blonde hair in need of a cut. In short, he was cut from the same god-like cloth as Tia's brothers. Too damn attractive for their own good.

Jack Orion held out his hand. Warm and dry and powerful, it nearly engulfed Tia's own.

"It's good to finally meet you, Ms. Smith. I find it hard to take the measure of a man—or woman—through email or over the phone. I prefer personal meetings myself."

Dark blue eyes studied her intently. Tia could see faint lines radiating from their outer corners—whether from laughter or sun exposure she couldn't say.

"Why don't we move over to the windows while we talk?" he asked. "I find the activity on the docks fascinating."

He still held her hand. She gently freed herself. "Whatever you'd like, Mr. Orion," she said, cool and polite.

She had read everything she could find on Jack Orion and his company before making this appointment. Nothing she'd seen so far contradicted her findings. Handsome, athletic, and very wealthy–in essence Orion was a man used to having things his way.

The society reporters loved him. He often graced their pages with a different–always beautiful–woman at his side, attending the orchestra, museums, gallery openings, regattas. One of Portland's most eligible bachelors, Jack Orion was a big fish in the city of Portland.

She followed him to the seating area and took one of the chairs. Crossing her long legs she waited to see how he intended to address her concerns. He surprised her when he didn't dive immediately into business.

"I often nap on this couch," he said as he settled onto it. "But please don't tell my receptionist. Ashely believes I'm in here working my fingers to the bone when I tell her to hold all calls. I'd hate to have her image of me ruined." His blue eyes twinkled, inviting Tia in on his little secret.

Damn if she didn't want to smile at him. She pressed her lips together and reminded herself why she had made the trip across town to his office.

"Mr. Orion–" she began.

"Jack, please. We'll be working closely together for the next three years. Mr. Orion will be tedious to say and to hear after one week. May I call you Tia? That's what your friends call you, isn't it?"

Tia frowned. Her first meeting with Jack Orion was not going as planned. He kept derailing her.

"Call me whatever you like, Mr. Orion. "There are several points I want to clear up before we actually begin working together. I don't know how much my father told you about the Bayside Project–"

"Enough to get me interested." What her father hadn't told him was how beautiful his daughter was.

"That's what I'm afraid of. He probably told you about the office buildings and condominiums and neglected to tell you about–"

"Excuse me a moment, Tia. I think I'd like some coffee after all. Can I have Ashley bring a pot and two cups?"

Tia took a deep breath and reined in her temper. "Thank you, that would be nice." She smiled sweetly. If any of her brothers had seen that smile they'd know to run and run fast.

Five minutes later she sat with a cup of coffee balanced on her leg. She took a sip of the dark roasted brew and waited to see if the man across from her was going to come up with anything else to keep her from saying what she came to say.

Jack drank his coffee while he studied Tia Smith. She was not at all what he had expected. He was used to beautiful women. They flocked to him and enjoyed his companionship. He could easily place them all in a mold–beautiful features, perfect form, lovely clothes and jewels, soft and feminine. The ones he dated more than once also possessed intelligence.

He had been surprised and intrigued when he shook Tia's hand to feel callouses on her palm. Most women who looked like Tia and had the money to do whatever they wanted had soft, weak hands. Hers had felt strong and firm. The hands of someone who actually did physical labor.

He found that strangely appealing.

Her physical presence filled his office. She had to stand nearly six foot in bare feet, with a lean, athletic body and a beautiful face framed by dark–nearly black–curls. Intelligence gleamed from her moss green eyes.

Those large eyes studied him now. He set down his coffee cup and leaned back on the sofa, put his feet up on the coffee table and prepared to spar with the lovely Tia. Anticipation made his blood quicken.

"So, you have a few points you wish to clear up before we move forward."

"Yes. I do, as a matter of fact. Did my father also tell you what I have planned to help with the housing shortage for the underprivileged?"

"He may have mentioned something about that being part of the project. We didn't get into details. He wanted to leave that up to you."

Tia stopped herself from rolling her eyes. Her father had a tendency to drop his children "in the soup" as they liked to say. He found it amusing to set them up in difficult situations so he could see how they wriggled out of them.

His children, on the other hand, were seldom amused by Father's little "lessons" as he called them.

"Oh, I think you must know more about my housing plan than you're admitting, Mr. Orion," Tia said mildly. "After all, didn't you leave a threatening letter and a cooler full of rotting fish heads on my doorstep?"

CHAPTER 2

JACK ORION NARROWED his eyes at Tia, any friendly feelings gone. Reputation was everything to him. He hadn't always had a good one–hell, he'd done a few things in his life he fervently wished he could erase–but he'd worked hard to change the world's perception of Jack Orion and he wasn't about to let Miss Tia Smith undo that with her false accusations.

"Is this some sort of joke?" he asked, his voice cool.

Tia set her coffee cup on the table with a sharp bang. "No, Mr. Orion, I certainly don't consider being threatened a joke."

A red and white Winslow tug caught her eye out the window as it carefully guided a barge loaded with construction equipment towards the Fore River. They were so close she could clearly see the men in the tug's wheelhouse.

The tug blasted its horn to warn everyone out of its way and Tia reluctantly brought her attention back inside. She needed to be out on her own construction site, not confronting an underhanded egoist in his posh office. Her anger grew.

"Why would I send you rotting fish?" Jack took his feet off the coffee table and leaned forward. "How could you accuse me of such a stupid act?"

Tia uncrossed her legs and leaned toward Jack until they were almost nose to nose. "Very easily, it seems," she answered. "I'm accusing you of the *stupid* act because of the nice letter you left with the fish. Did you think I wouldn't figure it out? Who else would want to scare me off my project? You want to swoop in and take it for yourself. Well, I'm here to tell you I don't frighten easily, Mr. Orion."

Jack held out a hand. "Do you have the letter?"

"Of course." Tia zipped open the worn canvas backpack she used instead of a purse and slapped a legal-sized envelope in his palm.

Jack took the letter to his desk where he pulled a pair of gold wire-rimmed glasses from a drawer and put them on. He slipped off his jacket and hung it over the back of his chair, then sat. He read the letter once, then a second time, before setting it on his desk.

Tia remained seated, watching him. There was something about those gold-rimmed glasses that she found attractive. Maybe it was because they made him more human, less than perfect.

Watching Orion frown over the letter, she couldn't decide whether he was a very good actor or if he had nothing to do with the fish heads and letter. Uncertainty took the place of the righteous indignation she had been carrying for the last twenty-four hours, but she was careful to keep her expression bland.

"This is a threat." Jack looked at her over the rim of the glasses. "It says if you don't scrap the plans for the Bayside project you'll be sorry."

"I know what it says," Tia answered, still irritated. "Are you denying that you sent it to me?"

Jack tossed his glasses on his desk and stood. "I don't play those kinds of games, Ms. Smith, and to be honest it pisses me off that you think I would. I have a reputation for being a straight shooter because I *am* a straight shooter. That letter was written by a coward."

Tia noticed he no longer used her first name. She watched him move to look out the windows. He put his fists in his pants' pockets and frowned at the tail end of the tug that was just passing.

Her gut told her Jack Orion was telling the truth. That was a good thing, since she needed Orion Development to help underwrite the costs of her project.

On the other hand, now she didn't know where the threat was coming from and that worried her. She set the problem aside to deal with when she had some free time.

Jack turned his head to look at her. With the sun from the window hitting the side of his face she could see that the light beard growth on his strong jaw was more red-gold than blonde. It was no wonder he had an endless stream of beautiful women hanging on his arm–he was very, very handsome and all male.

Jack definitely reminded Tia of her brothers. Big, masculine, too attractive for their own good, arrogant, and they loved women. Many women. She almost grinned, but smothered it just in time. She had Jack Orion's number. She could deal with him.

"Why would you want to work with someone who would resort to underhanded tactics like that?" Jack demanded. He jerked his head toward the letter on the desk.

"I don't," Tia replied mildly. "I came here today to tell you that our partnership is off the table."

Jack's eyebrows lowered. Now that he'd met Artemis Smith he wanted to know more about her. He had a feeling taking her to expensive restaurants and parties would hold little interest for her. The best way to spend time with this woman was to work with her.

He went on the attack. "You've already purchased the land."

"Yes, but–" Orion didn't let her finish.

"And you've already had all the surveys done and the site plans drawn up."

"Yes, but—"

He spoke over her again. "And I believe you've even begun the site prep for the first building."

Tia narrowed her eyes. If the arrogant SOB would let her finish her sentence she'd tell him that she had no problem working with him as long as he wasn't the one threatening her.

Triumph glowed in Jack's deep blue eyes. He moved in for the kill. "Given how far along you are, you need me, Ms. Smith. It's too late in the game to look for another source of funding."

Tia disliked arrogant men. Intensely. Unfortunately she had been surrounded by them most of her life. Jack Orion was just one more of a breed she understood very well.

"That's what I was trying to say, Mr. Orion." She used her cold, "you fool" voice, the one she pulled out whenever dealing with arrogant SOBs. "Since you aren't the one threatening me I'm happy to work with Orion Development."

She stood and walked to the door. "I've wasted enough time here. Why don't you meet me at the site and I'll walk you through how I plan to proceed. I'll be there the rest of the day."

She opened the office door and turned back. "It's never too late, Orion. If I learn you are the one threatening me after all I'll kill our deal immediately. In fact, if you read the last page of our contract, you'll see I've included a kill clause."

Stepping out, she closed the door with a firm click behind her, then strode past Orion's admin.

"Good day, Ms. Hayes. You'll need to clear some time in Mr. Orion's schedule for a site visit today." Tia never slowed until she was out of the building and standing on the wide, cement wharf.

She took a few minutes to take deep breaths and enjoy the Portland waterfront. The salt air carried scents of creosote, fish, fried food and diesel, all blended into a unique mix that only a working waterfront could produce. Black and white gulls called over her head. Two landed nearby looking for handouts.

Tia turned away and headed back to her truck. She felt good that she'd gotten the last word in with Orion. It was her experience that arrogant, handsome men needed to be handled in a certain way or they walked all over a girl.

As the only girl with three brothers, one of which was her twin, she had often suffered at the hands of just such men.

The day she had mixed florescent orange dye with her brothers' shampoo in retaliation for some trick they had played on her, her mother had taken her in hand and taught her a better way to deal with the boys.

She learned to ignore them and they eventually stopped tormenting her. As her twin complained to their mother, *"You spoiled our fun. Tia barely notices anymore when we do something to her."*

That didn't mean Tia let them get away with anything. Oh, no. She'd just gotten sneakier when it came time for payback.

The image of her three handsome brothers with neon orange hair still made her smile.

CHAPTER 3

THE DRIVE to the construction site from the docks involved either driving over the hump of land that was the Portland peninsula or taking the longer route around the city's east end. Tia turned right and followed the waterfront before cutting up to Fore Street.

Warehouses and loading docks gave way to businesses and restaurants before eventually turning residential. Fore Street turned into the Eastern Promenade, following the high promontory that marked the eastern edge of the peninsula with a spectacular view of the Atlantic and the Casco Bay islands.

The early city planners had wisely created an open green park between the road and the ocean, with plenty of room for residents and visitors to exercise and play, or even just to sit on the grass or one of the many benches and contemplate the view.

Large, original homes lined the opposite side of the road, well set back so they didn't crowd the promenade. Here lived the highly-paid professionals and those who inherited their wealth–the movers and shakers of the city–along with a couple lucky souls who's families had owned the houses when they were first built.

It wasn't always that way, she knew. For nearly a century, the hill leading to the eastern promenade, known as Munjoy Hill, was pastureland for the city's early settlers. As Portland's waterfront grew, so did the influx of the working class and immigrants–dockworkers who could only afford the cheap pastureland on which to build. The hill became notorious for its tough, close-knit, ethnic neighborhoods.

Today only the affluent could afford to buy those homes on the hill. Tia could do nothing to change that, but she could build affordable housing for the average worker. Which was exactly what she planned to do with her Bayside project. Bayside was the first of what she hoped would be a trend geared toward helping Portland's middle and lower classes.

She topped the hill and gazed out at the view she loved and visited nearly every day. The deep blue Atlantic sparkled in the sun, setting off the white sails of small J/boats out for an early race across the bay.

She liked to take her morning run along the promenade and often timed it to coincide with the sun rising behind the islands. The green and granite islands were often referred to as the jewels of Casco Bay. It was easy to see why.

Tia stopped to let a mother with three young children cross the road, then cut away from the promenade and headed for Back Cove. Like other port cities on the east coast, the edges of Portland's lone bay had been filled in over the centuries to provide new ground for expansion. Fortunately the area was closely regulated and retained much of its original charm. Tia often ran the footpath that edged the bay when she needed a change from the promenade.

That's how she'd found the building site and idea for her new project.

She pulled up at the Olympus Construction site ten minutes

after leaving Orion's office, pulled on her canvas messenger bag and grabbed her hard hat from the passenger seat.

This early in the process it was hard to imagine the entire complex of buildings that would grace the spot in five years time. At the moment it looked like a child's gigantic sandbox filled with earth-moving equipment.

She'd always preferred to play with her brothers' trucks over the dolls she received for gifts. Doing it for real gave her a rush that was hard to beat.

Great mounds of dirt were pushed up everywhere as two large bulldozers leveled and prepped the site for the first building in the mixed-use development, a six story commercial building for offices with ground floor retail, two restaurants, and penthouse apartments on the sixth floor.

Tia would have preferred to begin with the housing, but the city earned more taxes from commercial sites so she had adjusted her plans to keep the city officials happy.

As any structure was only as solid as its foundation, she was on site daily to make sure the company she had hired to sink the pilings that would support the building didn't cut any corners.

At first the workers had resisted her presence, giving short, unhelpful answers to her questions, but they eventually got used to her hanging around when they realized she wasn't going away. It helped that Tia held several Master Degrees, not only in Engineering, but also Architecture and Geology, and that she knew what she was talking about.

She also listened. She'd learned early in life that you learned more by listening than you did by talking.

Miles Angsley, the site foreman, called over to Tia as she walked away from her truck and came running toward her. She stopped and waited for him to catch up.

While incredibly handsome, there was something a little too perfect, too pretty-boy, about Miles' features for her taste. He fancied himself a ladies man, and to be fair, he seemed to date an endless string of attractive woman. A little like Jack Orion, Tia noted, although in her mind the similarity ended there.

Miles wore his dark, silky hair on the long side, tied back in a queue with a leather thong, something that struck her as a deliberate affectation.

On another man–Orion for instance–the queue would look right, like he tied the hair back to get it out of his way so he could get to work, not because he thought it looked sexy.

And why did she find herself comparing Miles to Orion? She had no personal interest in either man, they were only workmates.

Habit, Tia decided. She liked knowing which slot to fit people into.

"Good morning, Tia." Miles stopped next to her and smiled. His teeth were very white, almost too bright against his red lips. She wondered how often he visited the dentist to have them bleached, then pushed the thought away as being petty.

His brown eyes raked down her body and up again deliberately. Tia felt mildly irritated but ignored the look.

"Miles. Everything set for the pilings to go in today?" She turned away and started walking again to put a little space between them. Miles had a tendency to crowd her.

Tia didn't like being crowded.

"There's a new restaurant opening this weekend in the Old Port. Haggerty's. I was able to get reservations for Saturday night. How about you and me make the scene?"

"Thanks, Miles, but I'm busy." Tia had no interest in dating. Besides her mind being filled with work, all the men she knew seemed so needy. She had no desire to fill that need.

"You sure?" He reached out and ran a hand down Tia's arm. "You work too hard, Tia. You need to relax, have some fun. I can promise you we'll have some fun."

He looked deep into her eyes in a way she knew was meant to be soulful. Not wanting to insult her site foreman, Tia turned her laugh into a cough.

"Thanks, Miles, I'm sure you're an entertaining date, but honestly, I'm working seven days a week and at the end of the day I just want to put my feet up and zone out."

Miles dropped his hand. "All right then. But I warn you, I'm going to keep asking until you say yes. I think you and me could have a real good time together so I'm not giving up until you go out with me."

Tia spotted something moving across the site near a dirt pile. She squinted and looked harder. "Do I see something just in front of that pile of dirt?" she asked, pointing.

Miles turned and looked. "I don't see anything."

"I'm sure I saw something moving. Yes, there it is again. It's a dog." The dog was limping. No, she realized, it was dragging a back leg. Poor thing.

She altered direction and headed for the pile of dirt just as one of the bulldozers approached it from the opposite side. The dog saw her coming. Unaware of the danger, it began to climb the dirt pile to get away from Tia.

There was no way the dozer operator could see the dog struggling in the dirt from his vantage point. Tia waved her arms and yelled, but her voice was drowned out by the bulldozer's loud engine.

Tia sprinted toward the dog, visions of its suffocated, mangled body flashing through her head. She ran up the pile, sinking to her calfs in the dirt as she struggled to reach the dog before the bulldozer buried him.

Fortunately the poor animal gave up and lay on its belly. She could imagine it whimpering even though she couldn't hear a thing over the dozer, and her heart ached for it.

Reaching down, Tia scooped her arms under the dog and

lifted it to her chest, grateful that it wasn't a large animal. She turned and half fell, half scrambled down the dirt pile as the dozer began to push against it. Dirt rolled down the pile behind her, making her descent more difficult.

Tia landed on her knees at the bottom, struggled to her feet, and cleared the pile. The dog lay motionless in her arms. Fearing it was dead, she carried it back to her truck and gently laid it on the tailgate.

Tia ran her hand gently down the dog's painfully thin side. A half-grown male puppy, if she wasn't mistaken. The dog's ribs felt fine, but the odd angle of the left hind leg told her it was definitely broken. His short coat was matted and filthy, his long tail coated with mud and kinked and possible broken as well.

"Come on, fella, don't die on me. I just risked my neck for you," she crooned softly. She placed her palm against his chest between his front legs and thought she detected a heartbeat. Relief shot through her.

Miles came running up to her. "Tia! Are you all right? What a damn fool thing to do. You could have been hurt—or killed even!" He looked down at the dog and grimaced. "Disgusting, ugly thing. You should have just let the dozer bury it."

"He. It's a he, not an it. I'm taking it to the vet."

"Good idea. The vet can deal with it. I mean with him," Miles amended when Tia glared at him.

A horn honked behind them and a large, black SUV pulled up. Jack Orion stepped out of the vehicle and joined them.

"I don't have time for you now, Orion," Tia said, before he could speak. Rounding her truck, she opened the passenger door and looked at all the things she kept piled on the seat. Since she practically lived in her truck she really should buy an extended cab. She just never seemed to get around to it.

"What have we here?" Jack asked. "It looks like this little guy needs a vet."

"Tell me something I don't know," Tia snapped as she shifted the dog onto one arm and pulled a cooler from the passenger well with her freed hand. She swung the cooler into the truck bed.

"Forget that. I'll take you." Jack gently took the dog from her, wincing when it whimpered. "Broken leg, huh? Bet you met up with a car, didn't you? Missed a few meals too by the looks of it."

He turned his deep blue eyes on Tia. "You coming?"

CHAPTER 4

TIA STARED at Orion for a moment. Did she want him going to the vet's with her? She'd only met him a brief while ago. And he still could be behind the threats, she had only his word that he wasn't. His word–and her gut instinct.

Behind them, the bulldozer roared as it shifted the dirt that had almost buried the injured dog. A power shovel stood waiting to expand the hole for the first set of pilings.

Watching the first supports go in had become a ritual for Tia, one she never missed. She thought of it as her project good luck talisman.

Miles glowered at her from behind her truck. Beside Jack Orion the handsome site manager looked almost effeminate.

Tia made up her mind and gave a curt nod to Jack, then pulled a spare blanket she kept behind her seat and spread it over the cargo area of his SUV. "Lay him on here," she instructed.

She noted with approval that despite his large size, Jack was very gentle with the dog. She winced when the dog whimpered as he was set in the vehicle.

"Come on, fella. We're going to the docs. She'll fix you right up, I promise," she assured him as she stroked his sleek head. She prayed that her friend Cassidy could fix him up. If not, at least she could have the dog euthanized, a more peaceful death than the slow, painful one he faced on his own.

Miles stopped her with a hand on her arm as she climbed into the SUV's passenger seat. "Surely it doesn't take two people to take one small dog to the vet. You're needed here, Tia. Besides, it's just going to be put down anyway."

Tia narrowed her eyes at Miles until he dropped his hand. "Don't presume to tell me what to do, Miles. I'm sure you can manage for a few hours without me. I'll be back as soon as I can. I expect the first pilings to be well under way when I return."

She slammed the door and turned to Orion. "Let's go."

"Yes, ma'am." Orion resisted smirking as he drove past the furious Miles. He knew the site foreman slightly from other investment projects and neither liked nor disliked the man. Miles Angsley was capable and did the job. It was also obvious to Jack that the poor sod had the hots for his boss.

And who could blame him? Jack risked a glance at his passenger. Her delicate dark brows were furrowed over those amazing green eyes, whether in disapproval or worry, he couldn't tell. He didn't know her well enough yet to read her.

He intended to rectify that as soon as possible. He hadn't had a good puzzle to work out in too long.

"Do you have a vet in mind?" he asked.

"Yes, not far from here. Turn left onto Dartmouth. Cassidy's place is on the first block."

Jack did as instructed and parked in front of a large, three story home in a neighborhood of older, well-built homes. Tia was out of the vehicle before he engaged the parking brake. He opened the rear door and waited for her to pick up the dog who lay with his eyes closed and tongue out, taking shallow breaths. He could feel that the animal was near death.

"Where's the vet?"

Tia picked up the dog, blanket and all, and jerked her head at the large, three-story, green-shuttered, white house next to them.

"Cassidy's office is around back." Her throat had closed and her voice felt strangled. She could feel the animal's life force, his will to live, leaking away.

"Come on fella," she crooned. "I'm going to get you some help. You'll like Cassidy, I promise. She's the best vet in the city. Only the best for you."

She led the way up the path that circled the left side of the house and jabbed her arm onto a buzzer beside a wooden door painted dark green with "VET" in large white letters across its center. The buzzer echoed inside.

"Come on, Cassidy," Tia muttered, "we don't have much time." She heard footsteps, a viewing panel in the door slid open then snapped closed, and the door opened to reveal a small woman with a single blonde braid and pale blue eyes.

"Finally." Tia pushed into the room, barely glancing at her friend. "Is the OR free?" she asked.

"Just cleaned. What do you have?" asked the woman, looking at the blanket in Tia's arms.

"Young dog. Intact. Underfed, broken leg, possibly broken tail. Other injuries unknown."

Cassidy locked the door behind them and eyed the bundle in Tia's arms with an exasperated but fond smile. "Another one?"

"I can't help it. They find me, I don't go looking."

"I've heard that before. Come on in."

Forgotten, Jack followed the women through a small, empty waiting room with only two wooden captain's chairs, a scratched, wooden desk and a beat-up metal file cabinet. Nearly every inch of wall space was covered with photos of animals, mostly cats and dogs, although rabbits, birds, and guinea pigs were also featured. Many had smiling children and older adults in them. Most had "thank-yous" scrawled across them.

Light filtered through two pale green-curtained windows, casting the striped shadows of bars on the clean, dark green tile floor. Jack assumed the bars were there to keep out thieves. Like people doctors, veterinarians stocked drugs.

He looked out one of the windows but the view of the back yard was blocked by a wooden fence that most likely separated the vet's private space from her business.

The waiting room was neat and just shy of shabby. Either Cassidy wasn't a very successful vet or she didn't believe in pumping her wages back into her business.

Cassidy and Tia disappeared through the only door that opened off the waiting room. Jack stepped through behind them and blinked in surprise. Here was where the vet had spent all her money.

Bright white tiles covered the floor and walls. Stainless steel counters holding a pair of microscopes and other equipment he didn't recognize reflected the bright overhead lights. Rows of white cabinets lined the walls over the counters. A stainless table with drain channels running down each side sat over a floor drain in the center of the room.

"Set him on the table," Cassidy instructed Tia. "Let's get a look at you, fella." She checked the dog's heart rate, eyes, mouth, ears, and ran surprisingly delicate hands over his body.

Tia found herself holding her breath. She badly wanted this dog to live. Her friend seemed to be taking forever checking him out. "Well? Is he going to make it?" she asked impatiently.

Cassidy dropped her hands and shot a sympathetic look at Tia. "I don't know, Tia. He's severely dehydrated and hasn't had a decent meal in a long time, if ever. Add the trauma of the broken leg and—I just don't know."

"You'll do your best. Whatever it costs."

Cassidy smiled. "I always do, don't I?" She looked at Jack as if just noticing him. "Who's your friend?"

"My—oh. Cassidy, this is Jack Orion. He owns Orion Development. He's a potential investor in my Bayside project. Orion, this is my closest friend, Dr. Cassidy Reali."

"Pleased to meet you, Dr. Reali. Is there anything I can do to help?"

"I'd like you to wait in the other room if you don't mind, Mr. Orion."

"Or you could just take off," Tia added. "I'll get a taxi back to the job site. It isn't far. I could even walk it for that matter."

Tia didn't want Jack to stick around. If Cassidy had to euthanize the dog Tia would cry. She always cried when Cassidy lost an animal. She didn't want Jack to see her weakness, definitely didn't want to cry in front of him.

"Really," she said, forcing a smile, "I'll be fine. Thank you for getting us here so quickly."

Jack smiled back, revealing a dimple in his left cheek. "I'll wait. I want to see how things turn out." He turned and left the room, closing the door behind him.

Cassidy reached up and pulled a retractable hose down. Checking the temperature of the water, she began hosing the dog off with a soft stream of warm water. Sand and mud sluiced down the table's channels and into the floor drain.

Tia gently rubbed the dog down with one of the soft, absorbent towels Cassidy kept on hand while her friend set up an IV and added antibiotics to it.

Tia kept stroking the dog's head, letting him know she was there. He seemed a little calmer to her. She hoped it wasn't because he'd given up the fight.

"I don't dare to anesthetize him to set his leg," Cassidy told Tia. "His heartbeat is too weak. I'm afraid that would kill him. I want to get some fluids into him, something to fight infection, and see if his heart rate strengthens. If it does then we'll set the leg."

What her friend didn't say was that if the dog's heart rate didn't improve there was no point in setting the leg. Tia knew that, and ignored it.

"You can set it without anesthesia?"

"You'll have to hold him down. Or we could get Jack back in here to help. He's what my mother would call a big, strapping man." She looked at Tia, her blue eyes twinkling. "Quite a hunk of man-flesh, isn't he? Are you two dating?"

CHAPTER 5

Tia glared at her friend. Yes, she had noticed that Jack Orion was an extremely attractive hunk of man, but she was far too busy to even think about dating a man, let alone getting involved with one. Nor had she ever been. Especially not a business partner. Building her company took all her energy. She didn't have anything left over to stroke and build a man's ego.

Not that Orion had exhibited even the slightest personal interest in her. And why should he? Tia had seen the photos of him with beautiful women on his arm. After her father had told her that he'd approached Orion as a potential investor Tia had found scads of pictures, all with exotic, beautiful women who dressed to the nines, wore jewelry and makeup, and stuck arch-breaking high heels on their feet.

Tia couldn't remember the last time she had dressed up, let alone wore heels. She hated the things. She towered over most men already, she didn't need any more height.

When had she last found a good enough reason to dress up? She thought back. Oh yeah, her brother's wedding last year. And the time before that was another brother's wedding the year before that. She just wasn't a girly girl. She preferred construction sites and jeans and boots.

Much to Tia's continued embarrassment, Cassidy, who was happily married to a great guy and had three young boys, had always taken an avid interest in Tia's love life. Or more accurately, lack of.

"No, we are not dating," Tia told her friend firmly now. "And I doubt that we will after I accused him of leaving rotting fish on my porch along with a threatening letter." It felt gratifying to see the twinkle in her friend's eyes replaced by alarm.

"Artemis Smith! What are you talking about? Who is threatening you and why haven't you told me?"

Tia kept stroking the dog's head. Now that some of the dirt and clay had been washed away she could see that his short, smooth coat was a deep red color that reminded her of aged mahogany, mixed with black and brown. A black and red brindle? How unusual.

"Tia." The warning in Cassidy's voice was clear. "Tell me exactly what happened."

"When I left the house for my run this morning I found a cooler on the porch with a letter taped to the lid. The cooler was filled with rotting fish heads."

"Ew. That must have smelled good. And the letter?" Cassidy used her stethoscope to listen to the dog's heart and breathing and nodded, satisfied. The animal was hanging in there and even seemed to be gaining.

The strength of an animal's will to live never failed to surprise her. Especially if that animal knew that someone cared. She saw sick and injured animals who should pack it in recover and live many more years when they had owners who loved them.

Tia often brought Cassie abandoned and injured animals to fix up, then found good, loving homes for them afterward. She'd lost count of the number years ago, but many of their pictures papered the waiting room walls.

She would never say it to Tia's face because it would embarrass her friend, but Cassidy secretly thought of her as the patron saint of lost and injured animals.

"The letter?" she prompted. "What did it say, Tia?"

Tia's mouth tightened. "The letter said that I would be sorry if I didn't drop the Bayside project. That I could end up in a cooler, just like the fish heads."

Cassidy's eyes rounded in shock. "That's–that's a pretty serious threat, Tia. Have you reported it to the police?"

"Not yet."

"Why on earth not? What are you waiting for?"

Tia's hand stopped stroking. The dog gave a tiny whine, eliciting the ghost of a smile from her. She placed her hand gently on the dog's neck. "Like I said, I thought that Jack Orion was the one who left the cooler and letter. I wanted to confront him, tell him I wouldn't play that game, before I went to the cops."

"And?"

"And I no longer believe that Orion left the cooler or letter," Tia admitted.

"So. . . let me see if I understand the situation," Cassidy said slowly. "There's an unidentified crazy guy out there threatening to kill you and leave you rotting in a cooler unless you drop the Bayside project. The same project you've spent nearly every day of the last three years planning and pulling together." She looked at Tia expectantly.

Tia shrugged again and nodded. "Yeah. That's pretty much it in a nutshell."

"And you haven't reported the threat or taken precautions."

"Nope."

"You're nuts, you know that, you don't you?"

Tia looked down at the young dog and pondered her friend's

words. Was she nuts? She had actually been working on the Bayside project closer to four years than three, four years of architectural drawings, cost analysis, planning board meetings, permit applications, more meetings and revised drawings–a long, long process to pull together her dream project–but she had never lost heart.

What she planned to build would add attractive buildings to the city of Portland's growing landscape and fulfill several needs for decades to come. Bayside was not only a project she felt proud of, it was one she felt compelled to create. Whoever was trying to scare her off was going to be disappointed. She had no intention of quitting, especially not now when the actual construction was getting underway.

"Tia?"

"What?" Startled, Tia looked at her friend.

Cassidy glared at her friend. "I asked you what you planned to do about the crazy guy out there threatening to kill you and leave you rotting in a cooler unless you drop the Bayside project."

Tia frowned. "I don't know. Ignore him I guess. I can't quit now."

"You've never been a quitter. But I'm not sure that ignoring a serious threat is the answer, and leaving you rotting in a cooler sounds like a serious threat to me."

"I'll deal with it, Cass, I promise." Tia wanted to get her friend onto another topic. She indicated the dog. "Will he make it?"

Cassidy checked the dog's heart again. "His heartbeat is stronger. It looks like you got him here in time."

She smiled at Tia, a familiar glint in her eyes. "Well, if Jack Orion isn't the bad guy, then you can date him, right?"

Tia laughed, losing some of the tension she'd been carrying around ever since finding the cooler on her porch that morning. "You're a piece of work, Cass. You never give up."

"No, I don't. You deserve to have a good man in your life. Call your hunky friend back in here and let's see if we can get this leg set and in a cast. I have appointments the rest of the day."

Tia fetched Jack and between the three of them they quickly got the dog's broken leg set. Cassidy wrapped a cast around it and pronounced it was the best she could do.

"What about his broken tail?" Tia asked. "Can you fix that too?"

Cassidy peeled off her rubber gloves and dropped them in a covered bin. "There's nothing wrong with his tail. I can't be sure, but I suspect he most likely has some Rhodesian Ridgeback in him. Kinky tails are a genetic fault found in a small percentage of Ridgies. He appears to have inherited it along with the smooth coat."

"You think he's a Ridgeback?" Tia asked.

"No. He's a mutt, like all the others you bring me." She looked at her friend who was still stroking the dog's head. "What will you do with him now, Tia? You can't have him adopted until he's healthy. It wouldn't be fair to his new owner."

Tia looked down at the sleeping dog. "I have room. I'll take him home with me until the cast comes off. Then I'll look for a new home."

Cassidy nodded. "Fine. Pick him up tomorrow. I want to keep him overnight. That'll give you a chance to get dog food and a bed for him." She grabbed a bottle of pills from a locked cabinet and handed them to Tia. "Antibiotics. I'll pump more into him tonight with the IV fluids but he'll need these for the next ten days."

Tia took the pills. "Add them to my tab. I'll pick him up at the end of the work day tomorrow. Call me if he goes downhill. I'll come right away."

As they climbed back into the SUV so Jack could give her a ride back to the job site, he asked, "What's intact?"

"What?" Tia turned a puzzled frown on him.

"When we first got here you described the dog to your friend. One of the terms you used was 'intact'."

Tia smirked. "He hasn't been cut yet."

"Cut?"

"Fixed. You know, neutered. He still has his balls."

Jack winced and Tia laughed. "I have any animal I find a home for neutered first. There are too many unwanted animals in the world already without adding more."

"Why did you ask Cassidy to call you if the dog goes downhill? What could you do?"

"Nothing," Tia answered quietly. She looked out the side window so he wouldn't see the tears she felt gathering in her eyes. "I could do nothing. But he shouldn't die alone. He should have someone there who cares. I care."

They didn't speak again until Orion dropped her off and they agreed to meet later in the week at the site.

CHAPTER 6

WHEN TIA RETURNED from her run Thursday morning she found an unexpected visitor sitting on her front porch. He stood as she climbed the steps and handed her a bottle of water.

"What are you doing here, Orion? And how did you know where I live?" Tia's pulse gave a little flutter–surely her heart rate was elevated because she'd just been for a run. Or because she hadn't expected to find anyone on her porch. It couldn't be because she actually felt pleased to see the man.

She frowned, then relaxed. Seeing her as she was now–sweaty, panting, her hair a wild mass of black curls–was surely enough to put any man off.

It wasn't that she didn't like men, she did. She just didn't need one in her life. Growing up with her brothers she knew only too well the inner workings of a man's mind and she had no desire to play the part of some man's arm candy, to be shown off like a prized possession, admired and then tossed aside when a better piece of candy came along.

She had more important things to occupy her time. Like getting the Bayside project off the ground. "Our meeting isn't until ten, Orion. It's only seven." She looked at the offered water, then took it with a grudging "thanks".

"I realize you weren't expecting me." Jack forced himself to look away from Tia's long, unexpectedly tanned, and very shapely bare legs. Her tee shirt, damp from sweat, clung to her lean torso and hugged her perfect breasts. The woman was incredibly sexy, even if she usually dressed like a construction worker. He pictured her in a long, body-skimming gown. She'd look spectacular.

"So? What are you doing here?" Tia repeated. She glanced at the scratched face of her watch, a sturdy, no-nonsense model that could stand up to the rough treatment it received. She badly needed a shower and had planned to get to the site early today. Time was a'wasting.

"I wanted to see the dog." Jack knew she wanted him gone but he had no intention of leaving just yet. "I called Cassidy when I got back to town and she said he pulled through the night and had been released into your care."

"Oh." She hadn't expected Orion to even think about the dog after he'd dropped her off at the site, let alone care enough to follow up on him.

"Have you named him yet?" Jack sat back down in the wooden Adirondack chair and stretched his legs. He was dressed for a site visit in jeans, steel-toed boots, and a faded blue tee that snugged against his well-developed chest and tanned arms.

Tia noticed that Orion's arm hair had the same red-gold tint as his beard. She made herself look at his face, and saw that his eyes were twinkling at her. He knew she wanted him gone. She clamped down on the smile that threatened. She had no intention of encouraging a playboy like Orion.

"I named him Dozer," she answered, leaning against the porch rail. She opened the water and took a drink. The cold liquid slid down her throat and tasted great.

"Dozer?" Jack had a hard time taking his eyes off that lovely long, smooth throat.

"Because he was almost killed by one and because he sleeps a lot, although I suspect that's mostly due to his body healing."

"Dozer," Jack repeated, and smiled. "Good name. Can I see him? Or are you bringing him to the site with you?"

Tia shook her head. "Not yet. He isn't strong enough. According to Cass he should be up for visiting the site with me in another week. I come home for lunch to check on him and let him out."

Jack smiled again, this time exposing the dimple he knew women loved because many had told him so. "So, can I see him then?"

Tia scowled at him and his smile turned real. He enjoyed riling her although he wasn't sure why that was–he usually preferred to charm women. Something about Artemis Smith brought out his playful side, something he rarely indulged in.

"I suppose," Tia grumped, her tone anything but gracious. Her mother would have a fit if she heard the way her daughter was treating Orion. She pushed her always-correct mother from her mind, pulled a key from her shorts' zippered pocket, and inserted it into the door.

From the outside her house looked like a modest, older, three story home, one that had originally held a flat per floor, with the deep porch set across the entire front. Tia had bought the place three years earlier after the bank foreclosed on the landlord's loan, and had been renovating it on her own since. Hence the callouses on her hands.

"I have to admit I expected something . . . larger. More grand," Jack said as he stood behind Tia. She smelled of delicate female sweat with an undertone of sandalwood and a light floral note. Nice. "Which floor is yours?"

"All of them." She wished he wasn't standing so close to her. She felt crowded and found it difficult to ignore.

She suddenly felt nervous about letting Orion into her home. Very few friends had ever been inside–in fact, only Cassidy's family and Tia's parents had seen more than the front porch of her home. That was the way she liked it. Her home was her sanctuary, a place to get away from the world, not a place to entertain guests. That's what bars and restaurants were for.

She sighed and accepted that today Orion was going to get his way. He'd come for Dozer, she reminded herself, and she couldn't deny a person who cared about animals.

"Dozer, it's me," she called as she opened the door and stepped into the entry hall. She heard nails scrabbling on tile floor and then Dozer came charging out of the room at the end of the wide hall and barreled toward Tia. His cast barely slowed him down.

"Hello, handsome," Tia crooned as she knelt and gathered the dog to her chest. He licked her face and made happy dog noises, then realized she wasn't alone and growled.

"He seems to have bonded with you," Jack commented. He sat on the floor so he wouldn't tower over the dog and waited for Dozer to check him out. While he waited he looked around the entry.

It was more a room than a hall, with wide oak floorboards that had been stripped and refinished, wainscotting that had been painted a pale sage with cream-colored walls above, an oak staircase on the right that led up, and two large windows that looked onto the front porch.

Rows of wrought-iron hooks to the left of the door held a variety of jackets, coats, hats, and scarfs, and boot trays held Tia's outside footwear. Two doors opened off the entry–the one Dozer had come through and one in the center of the left wall.

There was no art on the walls or any sort of decoration to give him a better sense of the homeowner. Interesting.

Jack wondered what lay beyond each door but decided he wouldn't push his luck today. There would be plenty of opportunity to see more of Tia's house–he felt confident of that. Instinct told him he needed to move slowly with her or she'd shut him out of her personal life.

He had picked up on her nerves when he stood behind her on the porch. Tough. She'd have to get used to him. He wouldn't push, but he wouldn't back down either. The hunt was on and he fully intended to bag his prey.

He damn sure wasn't going to let her shut him out. Tia Smith was the most interesting woman he'd met in a long time–with the potential to be the most interesting woman he'd ever meet.

"Hello, Dozer," he said quietly. "What a handsome pup you turned out to be now that you're all cleaned up. Unusual color, isn't he?" he remarked to Tia.

Tia ran her hand down Dozer's smooth back. She could still feel every vertebrae and rib, but he had started putting on weight, eating everything she gave him and wanting more.

"He is unusual. If he was a horse he'd be a bay, with that deep red-brown body and black boots and ears. He seems to have a great personality. Once the cast comes off I'll begin walking him to build up the muscle. Cassidy's orders."

Jack reached out a hand, palm down so as not to be threatening. "Hello, Dozer," he repeated softly. "You're going to be a handsome boy, aren't you? And big too, judging by those enormous paws."

Still under the safety of Tia's hand, Dozer stretched forward until he could sniff the offered hand. He gradually inched away from Tia and sniffed Jack's legs, then his body. When he'd finished he returned to Tia's side and leaned against her.

"Looks like you've found yourself a dog," Jack remarked.

"Oh, I can't keep him," Tia said, rubbing one of Dozer's silky ears between her fingers. "I work seven days a week. I'd never be here for him."

Jack shrugged and got to his feet. He'd been here long enough. Tia was a bit like the animals she rescued. She needed time to get used to him and wouldn't appreciate being crowded.

"So take him to the job site with you. He'll get used to it. I'll let you get ready for work. We still on for ten at the site?"

"Yes. I'll see you there." Tia opened the front door to let him out. "Thanks for checking on Dozer. That was thoughtful of you." She closed the door behind Orion and roughed up Dozer's fur. He licked her hands. His eyes seemed to smile at her.

"What do you think, Dozer? Would you be happy living with me?" Dozer gave a single bark, making Tia laugh.

It would be nice to have company, she had to admit. Lately she'd felt that maybe, just maybe, her life needed something more than work. There was Tuffy, a feral neighborhood cat she fed on the back steps, but Tuffy never came inside and had only recently allowed Tia to scratch his scarred and battered head.

With the unknown person threatening her it might be smart to have a dog on the premises who would bark if anyone tried to enter her house. Dozer had a good bark, big and deep enough to scare off an intruder.

She had never before considered keeping any of the strays she rescued, but somehow keeping Dozer felt right. Maybe because she had literally saved his life at the last moment. Didn't someone once say that saving a life made you responsible for that life?

"Time for my shower, fella. I'll be down in a few minutes." Dozer couldn't navigate the stairs with his cast and Tia hadn't worried about it before today because he was only a guest. But now that he was going to stay she'd have to teach him how to climb the stairs. And run with her. And ride in her truck.

Tia was grinning as she raced up to her bedroom to get ready for work.

CHAPTER 7

Three weeks passed without incident. Mountains of earth were moved around the building site and the foundation of the first structure slowly began to take shape. For Tia, this phase always seemed to go on forever. It looked as if nothing was happening, and then suddenly a building began to grow out of the much-moved dirt.

Although Dozer had one more week until Cassidy removed his cast, once Tia had decided to keep him she began to take him with her everywhere she went. She cleaned off the passenger seat of her truck and rigged the seat belt so she could belt him in. In her mind, if it wasn't safe for people to ride without a seatbelt then it wasn't safe for dogs either.

Dozer loved riding in the truck and raced Tia to the door in the mornings, knowing he would be going with her. They quickly became inseparable, except at night since Dozer still couldn't climb the stairs.

On the Monday of the fourth week Tia arrived at the build site and found Miles and the equipment operators standing around waiting for her.

"What's wrong?" Tia asked, striding up to them with Dozer at her side.

Miles scowled down at the dog, then looked at Tia. "Someone got into the build site over the weekend and slashed the tires on all the equipment."

"What? Slashed the tires? How did they get in?" The build site was surrounded with an eight-foot chainlink fence posted with No Trespassing signs every fifty feet and security lights were left on at night to discourage vandals. The fence could be scaled, but not easily.

"They cut the fence at the back end, away from the road."

"Show me."

Anger and worry warred inside Tia. At one thousand plus dollars a tire, the cost to replace the slashed tires would be significant, depending on how many were ruined. Add to that the wages that had to be paid even if the men weren't working. She had a good crew and couldn't risk them leaving because they weren't getting paid.

"Every tire, Miles? Are you sure?"

Miles nodded, his mouth grim. "I'm sure. I checked them myself. I already called around the city to see how fast we can get them replaced. We'll be idled at least a week."

Tia groaned. Any building project had a time line that had to be met for funding to be released. While she always scheduled in extra days for the early stages of a project in case of bad weather or unforeseen problems, she had a reputation for wrapping up each stage early. Banks loved her for that.

Waiting around for tires to be replaced would eat up those extra days. Unfortunately they couldn't jump onto another area of the project because until the foundation was laid there was nothing else to do.

Was there a note?" she asked.

"Funny you should ask." Miles pulled an envelope from his jacket pocket and handed it to Tia.

"Did you read it?"

"Nope. It's sealed and addressed to you."

Tia took the envelope and tucked it into the back pocket of her jeans to read later when she was alone.

"Aren't you going to read it?"

"Not yet." Miles gave her a funny look but Tia ignored it. They reached the back fence and she looked around, trying to picture how it would look at night. A narrow strip of woods beyond the fence separated the build site from the back end of a mixed residential/commercial neighborhood.

"No one would notice them if they parked at a business closed for the night and came through these woods." She inspected the hole in the fence–the vandal or vandals had cut a four foot slice into the links, pulled the edges back, and slid right through.

"Quick cut through the fence. In and out in under ten minutes. Even with the night lights the odds of them getting caught were small." She shook her head in disgust. "Stupid. I should have hired a night watchman."

"We've never needed one before," Miles reminded her. He stood with his hands in his leather jacket pocket, staring at the cut fence. "Why do you think we need one now?"

"Bigger project. I don't think slashing the tires was some spur of the moment prank. Someone came here over the weekend prepared to do damage."

They turned away from the fence.

"Here, Dozer. Let's go, fella." Tia patted her leg, a signal for Dozer to join her, but he was sniffing intently at something near the damaged section of fence.

Tia changed course. "What do you have little guy?" she asked and bent down. The imprint of a large boot showed clearly in the soft ground. Tia roughed up the dog's ears and praised him.

"Have you called the police yet?" she asked Miles as she rejoined him.

He shook his head. "Nope. Waited for you."

Tia pulled her phone out of her pack and placed the call. "Oh, and tell them we have a clear boot print of whoever broke in," she said before disconnecting. "They might want to make a cast of it."

Miles raised his eyebrows. "They left a footprint?"

"A nice clear one. I want you to get the tires ordered and scheduled for replacement. No delays. Tell the crew they have four days off *with* pay. Emphasize with pay so they don't go looking for work elsewhere. Get the tires here ASAP. Don't take any excuses. If Portland can't supply them check Bangor. Or Portsmouth. Even Boston if you have to. I want them replaced by Thursday. I'll be back later."

"Where are you going?"

Tia knew she'd have to tell Miles about the first threat at some point but she felt reluctant to say anything at the moment. She had a feeling the envelope burning a hole in her back pocket was another threat. This time she would have to tell the police.

The first threat hadn't caused any harm, just some very smelly fish to get rid of. This one was far more serious and needed to be treated seriously.

Miles frowned at her. "Aren't you going to wait for the cops?"

"I have some business to attend to, Miles. They can call me if they have any questions that you can't answer. Once you get the tires straightened out you might as well take today and tomorrow off as well. Call me later with the tire schedule. I'll see you back here on Wednesday morning."

Tia didn't give Miles a chance to argue with her. She took off for her truck at a slow jog with Dozer hobbling beside her. The crew gave her a few nods as they passed her on their way off the site. She raised a hand in return and stopped to speak to Gus, a dozer operator she'd known for years, reassuring him that they would be paid until the equipment was operational again.

Many construction workers were transitory, drifting from one job to the next, following the work and the weather in the way of migrant workers. The operators who laid the foundation would move on once that phase was finished, but Tia paid them well to ensure they'd return when it was time to erect the next building.

She didn't have enough projects going to give the foundation crew steady work year-round, but most of the crew showed up for every project and she felt responsible for them.

Fastening Dozer into his seat, Tia followed her crew out of the gates just as a police car turned onto the road. For a moment she hesitated, wondering if she should return and talk to the police herself, but she decided against it. Miles could handle filing a report.

Tia drove to Cassidy's and parked the truck out front but didn't go in. She stared through the windshield at the large, leafy trees that lined both sides of the road, their branches meeting in the middle to create a shady, green tunnel. It was an excellent neighborhood, the homes and yards well-kept, with very little traffic. Her friend had done well for herself.

She really couldn't put it off any longer. With a sigh, Tia took the envelope out of her back pocket and looked at it. Despite the warm day, her body felt chilled. Goosebumps broke out on her bare arms. She knew the envelope contained another threat—she didn't even have to see her name typewritten on the outside to know that.

Her hands shook slightly as she ran a finger under the flap. Too late, she thought about fingerprints. She had handled the envelope and Miles had handled it as well—the likelihood of the police being able to get a decent print other than theirs was slim.

And now that she was thinking it through, she probably should have handed the envelope straight over to the police.

Too late now. Tia blew into the envelope and turned it so the folded sheet of paper inside fell into her lap. Handling it carefully by its edges, she nudged it open. As she had expected, the envelope held another threat.

THIS TIME WE SLASHED YOUR TIRES
DROP THE BAYSIDE PROJECT
OR NEXT TIME WE SLASH YOU

TIA REREAD THE NOTE. Short and to the point. It's ugly message made her skin crawl and a greasy ball of fear and anger settled into her belly.

"Great. Just great." Dozer looked over at the sound of Tia's voice, one ear cocked. "Since they are explicitly threatening me with bodily harm I guess I really do need to take this to the police."

Apparently her dog didn't see that as a problem. He looked back out the window, watching a young couple walking down the sidewalk toward them.

Tia shoved the note onto the dash but made no move to start the truck. She suddenly felt bone weary. She leaned her head back against the seat and closed her eyes. Did others have this kind of trouble with their projects?

She had fought for four long years for the Bayside project—finagling, cajoling, and changing her plans uncountable times to make everyone happy. When she finally got the go-ahead she thought it would be smooth sailing, other than the usual hang-ups that happen on a complex build like hers.

She never in a million years expected to be physically threatened. The problem with going to the police with the threats, the real reason she had not, was that her father would get wind of it and send her brothers to fix it.

The last thing she wanted was for her brothers to swoop in and take over, something they had a tendency to do. While they still pulled pranks on her at every opportunity, they were also fiercely protective of their only sister.

"Crap, Dozer. What are we going to do?" At least she was a "we" now. Well, sort of. If having a relationship with a dog counted. Tia sighed again. This time Dozer tried to reach over to lick her but the seatbelt held him. He whimpered.

"Right. Come on, Doze, let's go see if Cass is busy. I could use a two-legged friend right now." For some reason the image of Jack Orion's broad shoulders popped into Tia's brain.

"Not that kind of friend," she muttered as she released Dozer's seat belt. She hadn't seen Orion since the day she'd found him waiting on her front porch. They had met up at the site, looked over the plans, and he'd taken off. All communication since then had been through Ashley Hayes, Orion's admin/secretary.

Not that Tia had expected more. Orion Development had more balls in the air than just her Bayside project. Orion was a busy man. Besides his work, this was regatta season, and she knew that he was very involved with the local races held in the bay every Thursday evening. She had even taken Dozer for a walk on the promenade to watch the last two and followed the results in the papers.

Dozer waited for Tia to snap on his lead. He gave her hand a quick lick as she lifted him onto the ground. "Good thing that cast is coming off soon. At the rate you're growing I won't be able to lift you in another month."

Dozer seemed to smile up at her, making Tia laugh. The half-starved, nearly dead dog she had rescued was rapidly turning into a very handsome mutt. Best of all, he had oodles of personality and she already loved him.

Cassidy's front yard had blossomed into a riot of color since Tia's last visit. Giant blossoms of white, pink, and red peonies lined the walk, alive with bees anxious to gather pollen now that winter had passed. Dozer stuck his nose on a fat bumblebee. The bee buzzed and got barked at in return.

Despite her worries, Tia found herself smiling when Cass let her into the office.

"Tia! What are you doing here at this hour? Is something wrong with Dozer?" Cass's pale blue eyes filled with worry as she leaned down and ran her strong, gentle hands over Dozer's body.

"Dozer's fine." Suddenly Tia felt embarrassed to have bothered her friend. Cass ran a busy practice and got very few free moments. "Are you busy? I probably shouldn't have come." ·

Cass grabbed Tia's arm and hauled her inside. "Of course you should have come. I'm not doing anything I can't set aside for a few."

"If you're sure. I could use a cup of tea and an ear." Tia waited for her friend to lock the door behind her and followed Cass into the surgery.

Cass waited until they were both settled on stools with steaming mugs in their hands. Dozer was happily chewing on a knotted rope toy at Tia's feet.

"What is it, Tia? Something's happened."

"Someone broke into the build site over the weekend and slashed every tire on the equipment." Tia breathed in the bracing scent of peppermint before taking a sip. "They left a note."

Cassidy furrowed her eyebrows. "Someone vandalized the equipment and left a note? That seems fool—wait." She pointed a finger at Tia. "This has something to do with those rotting fish you found on your front porch, doesn't it?"

Tia nodded.

"What did the note say?"

"It said I'd be next if I don't quit the project."

The color leached from Cassidy's face. "Tell me you called the police."

"I called the police. Miles is dealing with them." She busied herself sipping the minty tea and watched Dozer.

"Ti-a. You didn't show them the note, did you? What's wrong with you, girl?"

"I didn't know what it said. I wanted to read it before I handed it over."

"That's bull. What's going on? Does this have anything to do with that hunky Jack Orion?"

Tia looked up, startled. "Orion? No. How could it have anything to do with him?" She slid off the stool and wandered over to one of the counters, careful not to touch anything on it. Dozer stopped chewing and looked at Tia, satisfied himself that they weren't leaving yet, and returned his attention to the rope. A dog's life was so simple.

"I've seen his photo in the paper's Sunday society section the last two weeks," Cass said, watching Tia. "He always has a beautiful woman on his arm."

Tia had seen the same two photos. And she'd noticed that Orion had the same beautiful woman on his arm in both of them. She turned to look at her friend and leaned against the counter.

"Jack Orion and I are just business partners, Cass. The vandalism has nothing to do with him."

"So why haven't you told the police about the personal threats?"

"Because my father will hear about them and he'll send my brothers." Tia scowled at the tea in her hand, then drained the mug and set it on the counter beside her. She wished she hadn't come to see Cassidy, especially when Cass hooted at her.

"Poor Tia. All those big, handsome men running to her rescue."

"I don't want—no, I don't *need* my brothers to rescue me. I can deal with this."

Cass's expression sobered. "I understand you not wanting your brothers to butt in, Tia, but it sounds as if whoever's trying to make you quit the project is getting serious. At least go to the police with the note, please. Your brothers are probably too busy to come anyway, at least right away. And ask Jack to help you find whoever's behind the threats. He has a vested interest. He'll help you get to the bottom of it."

Tia took a deep breath and let it out. "Right. I know you're right. I came here so you'd talk sense into me. I'll turn the note over to the police as soon as I leave here."

"And call Jack." Cass's eyes were twinkling. "Promise me you'll call Jack."

Ignoring her friend, Tia snapped Dozer's lead onto his collar and tried to take the knotted rope away, but he wouldn't let her have it. For a puppy he was already very strong. "I'll have to return the rope when he forgets about it."

"Keep it. Come by this Sunday and I'll remove the cast. We'll have a cookout. Dozer can meet the boys and get introduced to children. They'll love him."

She walked over to Tia and gave her a hug. "Don't worry too much, okay? You've put a lot into the Bayside project. Get some help dealing with the nutcase who's harassing you so you can get on with it and enjoy the building process."

A buzzer sounded in the outer room. Cassidy let go of Tia. "There's my next appointment. See you Sunday?"

Tia looked down at her friend. "Yeah, we'll be here. I'll bring potato salad."

A white-haired gentleman stood outside the door with a cat

carrier that hissed at Dozer as they passed. Dozer barked once and the man took a big step back.

"Does he bite?"

"Not that I know of," Tia answered. She felt herself smiling as she belted Dozer back into the truck. Even though he was just a puppy, he already possessed a big, deep bark. And Cass had told her that he was going to be the size of a small pony when he reached maturity, at least one hundred pounds. Possibly more. Anyone would think twice before messing with him—or with her when they were together.

"It was a lucky day for both of us when you wandered into my build site," she told the waiting dog and pulled gently at his ears. Dozer groaned in response and licked Tia's wrist.

She wasn't alone anymore. She and Dozer were fast becoming a team.

CHAPTER 9

Sunday broke bright and sunny with a light onshore breeze. A perfect early summer day on the coast of Maine. The promenade was bustling with runners, dog walkers, and parents pushing strollers, drinking coffee, and chatting up friends. The bay shone a deep, deep blue with dancing shards of sunlight on the crests of small waves.

Gulls wheeled and cried over Tia's head, keeping a keen eye on the people below for a dropped tidbit or an unguarded breakfast bagel. Tia nodded a greeting to the regular runners she saw every morning. People whose names she didn't know but faces she'd recognize on the street. Was one of them the person who'd been threatening her?

She kicked up her speed when she reached the turning point of her run where the promenade made it's turn and headed down to the working waterfront. She loved running, always had. As a young girl she'd run through the forests near her parents' home, either chasing after her brothers who didn't want a younger sister tagging along, or else running away from them when her brothers wanted to play a prank on her.

Concentrating on her breathing and memories and the

glorious morning, it took Tia a moment to realize that someone was running alongside her, matching her stride. She turned her head and looked into Jack Orion's smiling eyes. She couldn't help but notice that those eyes were nearly the same shade of blue as the bay that morning.

"Fancy meeting you here," he said.

"What are you doing here, Orion?" Tia put on a little more speed. Why, she couldn't exactly say. Maybe because it was something she'd do if she was running beside one of her brothers. Maybe it was because she didn't like that little jump her pulse made when she saw Jack Orion.

"I'm out for my morning run, like you," he answered easily. No way was he going to tell her that this was the third straight day he'd run on the promenade hoping to see her.

His long legs had no problem keeping up with Tia's stride. He had noticed her little increase in speed when she recognized him and responded to the challenge of it. He liked a challenge. Hell, he loved a challenge, and this woman represented the most intriguing one he'd had in . . . he thought back–ever.

Ever since he'd turned fifteen, Jack had never had trouble getting women. They made it too easy, like passing an exam designed for a first grader. All he had to do was smile at them and they offered him everything they had.

While flattering, over the years he had acquired a bone-deep cynicism where women were concerned. While he liked them well enough, nothing that easy to win over held much, if any, value for Jack.

The things Jack valued most were the things he'd had to fight for. Like building his business from nothing into the successful firm it was today.

A pair of pretty young women jogged toward them. As they passed, the blonde winked at him while her darker haired companion gave a soft "hubba-hubba." Jack ignored them. Since meeting Tia he had lost all interest in other members of the female sex.

Unfortunately he had made several commitments to the beautiful Tamara Allbrecht that he still had to keep. Tamara's family owned a large brewery in the midwest and had scads of money, some of which they'd invested with Jack's firm, including funds for Tia's Bayside project.

To be fair, Tamara was a genuinely nice woman. Just not his type. More accurately, she had stopped being his type after he'd met Tia. Tamara wouldn't be happy, but he intended to fulfill his social obligations to her and then gently part ways.

Jack knew Tamara was expecting a ring from him, and that was his fault. He'd made the mistake of mentioning that it was probably time for him to think about settling down and starting a family. He still felt that way, but now he was imagining a different woman playing the role of Mother.

"How's Dozer doing?" he asked Tia, pushing Tamara from his mind.

Tia had heard the hubba-hubba and seen the wink. She risked a sideways glance and wished she hadn't. Orion had stripped off his tee shirt, showing an impressive chest covered with a light mat of red-gold hair and ab muscles she could count. She felt her face flush and forced her eyes straight ahead, missing Orion's grin.

"Dozer's doing great," she answered cooly. Then, realizing she probably shouldn't be so short with her biggest investor, she added, "he's growing every day."

"Good. That's good. He's a handsome pup. I was wondering if you'd be free to have dinner with me one night this week? Say Thursday? I have a few questions about your plans for Bayside."

Actually he had no questions at all, but Jack felt fairly certain that Tia wouldn't have dinner with him if she thought it was a date. He watched her frown and knew his instinct had been right.

"Dinner? Oh–" she shook her head. "I don't think so. Why don't you just come to the site and we'll talk there?"

Dinner with Orion would be too much like a date and Tia didn't date. Never had. She knew too much about how men's minds worked and she wanted no part of their fantasies. She especially wouldn't date a man like Jack Orion, a serial dater who dated one beauty after another.

Besides, wasn't he involved with some wealthy socialite at the moment? She had seen multiple photos of him with the socialite draped all over him in the society pages over the past few weeks, even though she'd avoided admitting that to Cassidy.

Orion's feet slapped the running trail in perfect time with her own, their legs and arms moving in a matched rhythm. She'd never run with anyone before and much to her disgust found it exhilarating.

"I don't have time to visit the site this week," he told her. "Thursday night. I'll pick you up about six. We'll go somewhere nearby for pizza and I'll have you home and tucked in by eight. How's that sound?" He deliberately kept his tone brisk, businesslike.

Pizza wasn't really date food. Home by eight? She could handle two hours, and it would probably be even less if they were only having pizza. It certainly didn't sound like a date.

Tia made up her mind. "All right. Pick me up at six."

She slowed her pace for her cool down, said good-bye, and veered off the promenade, taking a side street she didn't usually take. She needed to get away from Orion.

Once home Tia sat on the back deck with her water and watched Dozer patrol the fenced yard. Cassidy had planted perennials along the solid wooden fence two years before as a belated housewarming present and she was pleased to see they were doing well. Purple, blue, and yellow irises had recently blossomed and fluttered in the breeze. In the left corner small brown birds flitted in a forsythia covered with small, yellow flowers.

She eyed the lawn critically and noted a few spots that could use another application of grass seed and organic fertilizer. Tia never used pesticides or herbicides. She fiercely defended every creature's right to live as they were designed to, and even released spiders outside when she discovered them in the house. She was incapable of killing.

Dozer leaped up onto the deck, avoiding the three steps that he couldn't climb because of his cast.

"Such a smart dog," Tia cooed, rubbing his ears. He allowed her a moment to love on him before seeking out the knotted rope that was never far away. Tia made a mental note to buy Cassidy a replacement–Dozer considered this one his and would never give it up.

She relaxed back in the wooden Adirondack chair and let the sun warm her face. Her thoughts turned to the threats against her and the Bayside project. Like Dozer with his knotted rope, the threats were never far from her mind.

Was it an individual or more than one person? According to Miles the police had not made a cast of the footprint Dozer had found, although they did measure and photograph it.

One man working alone could have punctured the tires in a fairly short period of time and would be unlikely to be noticed. Tia preferred to leave the heavy equipment neatly parked to one side over the weekends which had made it easy on the vandal. He just had to work his way down the line of vehicles. Could have even used them for cover while he trashed the tires.

She made a mental note to have the operators leave their machines where they sat at the end of every work day. No more striving to have her build sites look organized and squared away.

So, what did the vandal want? According to the two notes she'd received, he wanted her to back out of the project–that was painfully obvious. But why? What did he stand to gain? If she was going to find whoever was behind the threats she needed to discover what they were after.

Jack Orion invested in projects like Bayside—he didn't personally build them—so he had nothing to gain. He won no matter who did the build. Tia had pretty much knocked him off her list of suspects after the first threat but it felt good to reaffirm that. She didn't ask herself why. She didn't want to go there.

An image of Orion running next to her, sunlight glistening off the light film of sweat covering his chest and shoulders, flitted into her mind. She resolutely pushed it away.

There had been two other groups interested in the Bayside property, she remembered. They had made presentations to the zoning and planning boards similar to the ones she had made. Hers had been chosen over theirs, a real coup at the time because she knew the president of one of her rivals had some family connection on the planning board.

She had won because unlike her competitors who had gone with modern glass and steel structures, her proposed buildings were based on Portland's historic districts—faced with brick and granite, with cobblestone streets and brick sidewalks. Bayside would add to Portland's unique beauty, not turn it into a city like every other city.

If Tia walked away from Bayside one of those two groups would then be able to develop their project. That's where she needed to start looking for the vandal.

She knew just where to start. As a development investor Jack Orion would be familiar with the principal players of both rival groups.

She suddenly found herself looking forward to sharing pizza with Orion Thursday night. He might have questions for her, but she had some for him as well. Cheered by that thought, Tia headed inside to shower and dress for Cassidy's cookout.

CHAPTER 10

Tia had to park the next block over from Cassidy's street and walk to her friend's house with Dozer's leash firmly gripped in one hand and a large bowl of potato salad held tight against her body with the other.

On a beautiful Sunday afternoon the Back Bay neighborhood was alive in a way it never enjoyed during the week. Children rode their bicycles or chased after each other through their yards, screaming, laughing, and hollering at the top of their lungs. Exuberant. Full of life, the way children should be.

She heard the bounce, bounce, bounce of a basketball on hardtop and saw a group of teens dressed in baggy shorts and tees playing a game in a drive just ahead.

Dozer limped along right tight against Tia's leg, his head swiveling left and right as he tried to take it all in, his now much-frayed knotted rope held firmly in his jaws. Tia thought of the toy as Dozer's security blanket as he insisted on taking it everywhere.

She couldn't blame the pup for feeling intimidated, especially considering his background. Someone had booted the young dog out on his own. He had starved and had been hit by a car. Had he wandered this very neighborhood looking for food or a kind soul to help him? Tia's heart squeezed when she thought of how frightened and alone he must have felt.

"What a good boy, Doze," she crooned. He seemed to relax slightly but remained pressed against her leg.

Two young boys rode up to them on their bicycles and stopped. "What happened to your dog?" asked a gap-toothed kid with a shock of bushy black hair.

"He was hit by a car."

The kid gave Tia a stern look. "My mother says you're supposed to keep your dog on a leash when he's outside, or else keep him tied up in the yard. You should take better care of him."

Tia smiled. "That's good advice, kid. Unfortunately I found him after he'd been hit."

"Oh." The boys seemed to think about that a second, then raced off, yakking at each other, probably looking for someone else who needed their good advice. She chuckled at the thought.

The meeting with the boys had lightened Tia's mood. She smiled broadly at her friend when Cassidy opened the clinic door and shooed her inside.

"You look cheerful," Cassidy commented as she closed and double-locked the door behind Tia. "I'm glad you decided to join us. I'll just get that cast off and we'll head out back and join the boys. The yard is fenced all the way around so you'll be able to let Dozer sniff and explore. It'll give him a chance to get used to no cast."

Once the cast was removed and Cassidy had given Dozer a quick once over, Tia lifted him off the table and set him on the floor. He stood unmoving for a moment, bent his body so he could sniff at his cast-less leg, and took a tentative step. Two more steps and Dozer broke into a hunch-backed run, racing around Cassidy's surgery.

The two women laughed at his antics. "He's going to be a fine looking dog, Tia. And a good watch dog for you, I think. He's definitely bonded with you. Have you learned any more about who vandalized the equipment at your job site?"

Tia shook her head. "Nope. The police say they have no leads. Let's not talk about it today, all right? I just want to relax and enjoy your boys while I eat too much and have a beer."

"Fair enough." Cassidy tossed the smelly cast into a plastic bag and tied the bag closed before dropping it into a waste receptacle. "Len got a new grill and is excited to show it off."

Tia gathered up the potato salad and Dozer's lead. "Let's go then, I'm famished."

They took another door out of the surgery, one that led into the tiled mudroom of Cass's house, and from there made their way out onto a large wooden deck that looked over the back yard.

"Ooh, Cass. Looking good." Besides animals, flowers were her friend's passion. The high, wooden fence that enclosed the yard was footed with a continuous splash of color. Several large maple trees provided shady spots and separated the large yard from the neighbors. "What's that salmon colored patch over there?" Tia pointed at a spot to her left.

"Poppies. I seeded them in last fall, didn't know if they'd make it or not. I love the color."

"They're certainly bright. The irises you put in for me are blooming. They're gorgeous. I love them."

Cassidy nodded. "I used more subtle colors for your yard." She gestured toward the brightly colored poppies. "Those colors just aren't your style."

Cass grinned at her friend. "You know me so well. Now where's that handsome husband of yours? I want to give him a hug and tell him how lucky he is to have you."

Cass frowned. "I thought he'd be on the deck with his new

toy. And the boys. They're fascinated with Dad's shiny new toy. Where—" she was interrupted by the appearance of three young boys tumbling out of a wooden shed painted to look like a miniature house set in the back left corner of the yard. "There are the boys."

Before she could say more two men followed the boys out of the shed.

Tia turned to look. Her mouth dropped open when she saw a tall man duck out the shed's doorway. "What's he doing here?" she hissed at her friend. She narrowed her eyes. "Cass? Did you invite Orion?"

"Well, yes. Of course I invited him. You didn't think he'd just show up, did you? Jack is a nice man, Tia. He called to ask about Dozer and we got talking." She shrugged. "So I asked him if he was doing anything this afternoon and he said no."

Tia muttered something under her breath. The boys spotted her and came running for the deck.

"Aunt Tee! Guess what Dad's going to do?" The youngest boy, five year old Griffin, threw himself at Tia and hugged her legs. Dozer growled.

Tia reached down and picked Griffin up. "Oof. My god, Grif, you're growing so fast. I have to put you down, you're too big to hold anymore."

Griffin laughed with delight. All three boys had their father's black hair, warm brown eyes, and Italian good looks. Tiny, blonde Cassidy looked like an alien creature when surrounded by her menfolk, but Tia knew that Cass ruled the household and they all adored her.

All three boys lined up in front of Tia. Dozer scooted around behind her and pressed tight against the back of her legs, his rope gripped firmly in his mouth. She was pleased to note that he'd stopped growling and his tail gave a tiny wag.

"Who's that?" Seven year old Carter, the middle boy, pointed a dirty finger at Dozer. The boys were well acquainted with Aunt Tee's habit of bringing strays to their mother.

Tia knelt and put an arm around her dog. "This is Dozer. I rescued him and your mom fixed his broken leg. She took his cast off just a few minutes ago. He's a little nervous, but I think he'd like to meet you. Carter, you first. Come say hello."

"I know how to do it," Carter said as he stepped forward. "Mom taught us." He held out the back of one hand for Dozer to sniff.

While the boys introduced themselves to her dog, Tia couldn't help but be aware of Orion standing not far behind them, watching. From under her lashes she saw that he was wearing well-worn khakis, frayed at the cuffs. That surprised her. She'd pegged Orion for a bit of a dandy, one who always dressed well when in public.

She looked up and saw that he was smiling down at her. Her pulse did a little hitch, then steadied. Why the hell had Cass invited the man? Tia wasn't sure if she felt angry or pleased to see him. His presence had been unexpected and threw her off stride.

"Orion."

The smile widened and the dimple appeared. "Tia."

"Boys, why don't you grab a tennis ball and see if Dozer likes to play fetch," Cass suggested. "Dad will get the grill going so we can eat soon."

A chorus of "yays" erupted and the boys thundered off the deck with Dozer at their heels.

"You have nice boys, Cass. You must be very proud of them." Jack turned around to watch Dozer chase after the boys. "Dozer doesn't seem intimidated anymore," he observed as the boys tumbled and ran with Tia's rescue.

Jack knew from her reaction that Tia hadn't been expecting to see him. He could see the war between pleasure and displeasure in her eyes. He was glad to see the pleasure. It meant he was making progress. Getting Tia to go on a date was a bit like taming a wild animal. You had to take it slow, let her get used to you being around.

He placed a personal bet with himself. Another month he'd be taking her to dinner. A real dinner, not pizza, but a date dinner. The thought pleased him enormously.

Tia turned away from Orion's scrutiny and joined Cassidy's husband at the grill.

"Tee, it's so good to see you. You don't drop by anywhere near often enough," Leonard said as he gave her a bone-crushing hug.

Cassidy's husband stood several inches shorter than Tia's own six foot but he was strong and always gave good hugs. "Len, you're squeezing the wind out of me," she gasped.

He released the hug but kept his arm around her waist. She recognized the gesture for what it was. Leonard was telling her that no matter what, she had his support. Cass must have told him about her vandal and the threats.

She kissed his cheek and smiled fondly at her dearest friend's husband. Leonard was a gem among men and she felt grateful for his friendship, loved him like another brother.

"So," she teased, as she watched him fill the fire-starter chimney with charcoal and crumpled newspaper, "am I going to start seeing you on the BBQ competitions on television? 'Grill Master Leonard Reali demonstrates his superior hamburger, tonight at seven.'"

"Har-har. Get yourself something to drink and leave the master to it. And get Jack something while you're at it." He leaned over so no one else could hear and whispered, "I think my wife is trying to set you up again."

Tia made a face at him. Cassidy's only fault as far as their friendship went was that she seemed to be on a permanent mission to get Tia married. Tia had explained to Cass countless times–after every failed date, in fact–that her standards were impossibly high, and begged her friend to stop trying to fix her up. But Cassidy proved to be a hopeless romantic and refused to quit.

Well, at least Tia knew Jack Orion a little. And he *was* damned attractive. It wouldn't be a hardship to spend a few hours with him, especially in the company of the Reali family.

An hour later they all sat at the long picnic table eating. Dozer lay in the shade under the table at Tia's feet, snoring. The boys had worn him out. Orion sat beside Tia, his arm occasionally brushing hers as they ate and drank. Every time they touched she felt a little jolt. She tried moving away without being obvious about it but Griffin was sitting tight against her right side and she had no room to move.

Her potato salad was a huge hit, the burgers and hotdogs were grilled perfectly, the lemonade tart, cold, and refreshing. Overhead puffy white clouds sailed across the deep blue sky. A perfect summer day with friends.

The conversation around the table was relaxed and easy, as if they'd all been friends for a long time and there wasn't a stranger in the group. Tia had to admit that Orion had slid right in, playing ball with the boys, talking with Cass and Leonard. She found herself looking for something to find fault with but came up empty.

"What's the matter, Tee?" Leonard asked. "You're frowning at my hamburger. Isn't it done the way you like it?"

Tia flushed. "The burger is perfect, Len. No worries. I was just thinking about . . . " She searched around for a topic. ". . . work," she finished lamely.

"Ah, of course. I heard about the slashing. Do the police have any leads on the vandal yet? That must have cost you some bucks, replacing all those tires."

Tia felt Orion stiffen beside her. He set down his own burger and carefully wiped his mouth.

"What are you talking about?" He looked at Leonard, then down at Tia. "Has there been another incident that I haven't heard about? Tia?"

"I HAVEN'T HAD a chance to tell you," Tia answered. Why had she told Len she was thinking about work? Stupid. Now she was going to have to tell Orion about the latest threat and she wasn't ready. She wasn't sure why she didn't want to tell him—maybe because the threats made her look weak?

"Someone got into Tia's build site and slashed all the tires on the heavy equipment," Leonard told Jack. He stabbed another forkful of the potato salad. "This potato salad is awesomely good, Tia. You'll have to give Cass the recipe."

"Thanks, Len." Maybe Orion would let the subject drop. "I'll write it down for you before I leave, Cass."

"Ti-a. What happened?" Orion's gaze was steady on hers, his deep blue eyes angry. This close, Tia could see yellow rays in his blue irises. The fine crinkles at their outer edges didn't look so friendly at the moment.

Tia stifled a sigh. "I had planned to tell you about the vandalism when we meet on Thursday."

"Damn straight. We'll also discuss why you waited to tell me. I should be kept informed of any problems *when they happen*. Do you understand?"

Tia could hear the anger in Orion's voice even though he spoke softly. She almost squirmed in her seat, but she didn't want him to know that she knew she should have contacted him immediately. He had a vested interest in the project.

Why hadn't she informed him immediately? If she had she wouldn't be sitting here with her friends, feeling embarrassed.

She knew the answer, but she wasn't happy about it. She was avoiding Jack Orion. She was too aware of his masculinity and that made her uncomfortable. She kept trying to place him in the same category as her brothers but it was proving to be difficult, if not impossible.

The knowledge that she had been wrong to withhold information about the vandalism made her feel obstinate and defensive. Never a good combination. Before she could tell him there was nothing to discuss, Leonard spoke again.

"That's not all," he added, oblivious to the sudden tension at the table. "The vandal left a threatening letter addressed to Tia. Said she'd be next if she doesn't back off the project. Not that she ever would. Tia's put the last four years of her life into Bayside. Isn't that right, Tee–ow."

He rubbed his shin, then looked up and saw Jack glaring at Tia. "Uh-oh. I guess I should've kept my mouth shut. Sorry, Tee."

Jack Orion set down his burger and slowly stood up. He clamped a large hand on Tia's arm and pulled Tia to her feet. "Excuse us a minute, folks, we'll be right back. Come with me, Ms. Smith. We need to talk. *Now*."

Tia jerked her arm free. "You don't have to drag me." They stalked side by side toward the back fence. Dozer followed with his rope.

"Is Aunt Tee in trouble?" Tia heard Griffin ask behind her.

If he only knew.

"I think Jack's mad at her," Carter answered.

Smart boy. Orion was definitely angry. And she only had herself to blame.

"Aunt Tee can take care of herself." Alan, the oldest of the three boys spoke with all the confidence of a nine year old.

Tia hoped he was right. She could almost feel the waves of anger pulsing off Orion as he stalked next to her.

When they reached the shed they stopped and faced each other. Tia drew herself up as tall as she could and met Orion's angry eyes.

"Now, tell me what happened, Tia. Don't leave anything out. Not a dammed thing–I want the whole story."

Tia glared back at him, her own anger finally kicking in. If she'd been a man he would never have dared to treat her this way. Like a . . . mis-behaved child. Well, she wasn't a child and she didn't have to put up with being treated like one.

"Fine, Orion, I'll tell you. This past Monday when I showed up at the site the entire crew was standing around. Every tire had been slashed. I found a gap in the back chainlink fence where the vandal had cut a way into the site. Dozer found a good footprint. I called the police. Miles had found an envelope addressed to me. Inside was a note that said if I didn't drop the Bayside project I would be next. Satisfied?"

She crossed her arms over her chest. "Oh. And I told my operators I would pay them for the days they couldn't work and sent Miles to find me new tires, but don't worry, I'll make sure that all comes out of my profits, not yours." She didn't say it, but the word "asshole" hung in the air between them.

Jack took a deep breath and let it out, then ran a hand through his thick hair and rubbed the back of his neck. "You swear you planned to tell me all of this? On Thursday?"

Tia scowled. "Yes. I've been trying to figure out who's behind the threats and I can only come up with two possibilities–the two other companies who wanted to develop Bayside. They weren't happy when my design was chosen over theirs and I won the right to buy the property from the city. I figure you know all the players. You can help me find out who's trying to scare me off my project. The police don't have the time or the manpower to follow up."

She stopped talking and waited. She could hear Cass's boys asking when they could have dessert. A splash sounded on the other side of the fence. The neighbor must have a pool.

A cloud passed over the sun and the temperature dropped. The brightness went out of the day. The cloud passed and the sun came out again. All of it felt as if it was happening outside a bubble that surrounded her and Orion.

Meanwhile Orion said nothing. He just watched her, his expression unreadable. Finally he gave a small nod.

"You're right, I do know the players, so I'll help you figure this out. On one condition."

Tia stiffened. "What's that?" she asked cautiously. She had a feeling she wasn't going to like Orion's terms one little bit.

"I move into your house until we nail whoever's behind the threats. You must have a spare room I can use. It's gotten too dangerous for you to be alone."

Jack smiled inwardly. It was a dastardly, unreasonable request, one Tia would hate, he knew. But she had no choice. She needed his help to make the threats stop. He barely resisted rubbing his hands together with glee. A man had to take advantage of a golden opportunity when one presented itself.

"What?" Shock bloomed across Tia's features. Her curls bounced around her face as she shook her head. "No. Absolutely not. No. No. No. Besides, I'm not alone, I have Dozer now and he has a big bark."

"He does have a good bark, but he's still just a young puppy. My terms or you can forget my help. I might even pull my funding."

Jack didn't tell Tia that both were empty threats. He would never pull his funding and he would turn over every rock to learn who was threatening her, even if she didn't let him move in. Let her think she had no choice.

Part of Tia leapt at the idea of getting to know Jack Orion better. Another part–the bigger, stronger Tia who knew how to handle her brothers–abhorred the idea. Since moving away from her parents she'd lived alone. She didn't want a roommate. She especially didn't want Orion in her house, poking around her life.

"I'll come stay with Cass until we find out who's writing the notes."

"If you do that you could put her family in danger. Do you really want to risk that? What if whoever's behind the threats kidnapped one of the boys?"

"Crap." Tia scowled. She'd sacrifice her life before she put Cass's family at risk. "I hate this."

Jack could almost taste victory. He put a sympathetic expression on his face and nodded. "I know. I'm sorry, but unless you can hire a personal bodyguard you'll have to settle for me."

Tia's expression grew thoughtful. Had he blown it? Why had he mentioned a bodyguard?

Tia considered who of her family would be free to live with her for a while. The big problem was that she had no idea how long they would need to stay. She couldn't just ask them to move in indefinitely. Zee and Pandora had a young baby. Pauli and Cassandra were still honeymooning. She had no idea where Percy had gotten off to. He was always traveling.

She didn't have any male friends she wanted to live with, even for a short time. She could hire a bodyguard. But that would mean inviting a stranger to live in her house. Probably two strangers as she couldn't expect one man to work twenty-four/seven for her.

Tia narrowed her eyes at Orion. He had rolled up the sleeves of his faded chambray shirt and crossed his arms over his chest. Mimicking her? Mocking her?

"Fine. You can have a room on the second floor until–and only until–we find out who's writing threatening notes to me." She tapped his chest with her finger and was surprised by how solid he felt. She quickly stuck her hand in her pocket.

"There will be rules."

Relief washed through Jack though he was careful to keep his face impassive. Living in Tia's house would provide him with opportunity. He felt confident he'd be taking her out to a real dinner within a week. From there, it would be easy to get her into his bed.

The thought of Tia beneath him, naked, stirred his body, he took care not to show his thoughts. For now, he'd won the skirmish and he'd be satisfied with that.

"What rules?" he asked. He wanted to laugh out loud at the scowl on her beautiful face.

"I don't know yet," Tia muttered as she stalked away from him. "But believe me, there *will* be rules."

CHAPTER 12

TIA DUG her spare key out from under the back deck, let herself in the back door, and disengaged her security alarm. She had bitched and moaned at Dozer all the way home from Cassidy's about Jack Orion and was still steaming.

First thing she needed to do was get a new spare key made. She'd given Orion her key and made him memorize the security code so he could let himself in. As soon as this was over and he'd moved back out she'd change the code and the locks as well. Just in case the arrogant jerk thought he'd be clever and make a copy of her key.

Once inside, Tia fed Dozer and gave him fresh water, then headed up the rear stairs to the second floor. When she'd bought the building each floor contained a single two-bedroom apartment, complete with living room, kitchen, and bath. Tia had started her renovations on the first floor, removing walls, refinishing the old oak floors, and expanding the kitchen.

Other than the entry hall, the entire first floor was now an open, L-shaped floor plan, with the kitchen flowing into a dining space across the back of the house. The dining area flowed into the living area that ran down the length of the east side of the house. The living area could also be accessed through a door off the front entry which also held the main stairway to the second and third levels.

The living and dining areas got the morning sun, the dining area and kitchen received the daytime sun, and the late afternoon sun hit the kitchen, making the entire space warm and inviting from sunup to sundown. As Tia preferred being outdoors to being inside, letting in the natural world was an important aspect of her renovations.

She reached the landing to the second floor and headed down the wide hallway. The second floor renovation was more extensive and still in progress. Fortunately one half of the space was done as she'd needed a place for her parents to sleep whenever they visited.

The center hall now bisected what would eventually be two guest suites. She stepped through an open door on the left into a sitting room and ran a critical eye over the space. A quick dust and it would be fine.

A thick, red oriental rug covered most of the refinished oak floor. Two over-sized (her father was a big man) brown leather reading chairs faced a deep-cushioned couch. Several watercolors–gifts from her parents–of her childhood home, Mount Olympus, and the family's favorite villa in Italy, adorned the soft taupe walls.

She checked the large front bedroom with its massive king-sized bed. Everyone in Tia's family slept in a king bed. They were all tall and hated to be cramped.

The bed's down comforter stood neatly folded on the bare mattress, topped with several naked pillows. Tia went to the closet and pulled out a set of sheets and pillowcases, then tossed them on the mattress. Let Orion make his own bed.

She walked back through the sitting room and checked the bath and kitchenette. Both were stocked with essentials. She made sure the coffee maker had filters, then pulled a bag of coffee beans from the small freezer and set them on the counter next to the grinder. Orion could be responsible for anything else he needed.

Would he expect to take meals with her? She had no previous experience with roommates, even a temporary one, and had no clue as to the proper protocol. She scowled as she did a quick dust of the furniture and opened the wooden blinds.

Dozer chose that moment to make an appearance, obviously thrilled and pleased with himself that he'd negotiated the stairs. Tia squatted and hugged his wriggling body.

"You're such a good boy," she murmured. "I don't need that—that macho *oaf* staying here. I have you. We need our privacy." Dozer gave her a sympathetic lick, making her laugh. "Good boy." She rubbed his ears and then his soft, smooth tummy when he rolled over and offered it to her.

Feeling slightly better, Tia tossed the dust rag down the laundry chute she'd built into each bathroom and headed up to the third floor. This was her private space, and still under construction.

She'd knocked out all the walls here too, except the ones that enclosed the bathroom, which she'd enlarged into part of the smaller bedroom next to it and completely refitted with a glass and tile shower and a long, deep soaking tub. Eventually the rest of the small bedroom would become a walk-in closet.

After spending the day on a dirty construction site a hot soak after she'd washed off the surface dirt was often necessary. She'd installed a large skylight over the tub so she could look at the stars while she soaked. The skylight also let in plenty of daylight and made the bathroom bright and inviting during the day.

But her favorite feature of the bathroom, even more than the large tub with skylight, was the mosaic she had created on the walls. Stepping into her bathroom was like entering a forest glen with trees and leaves and sly, shy creatures peeking through the branches and around the trunks. She'd even added a pond complete with frogs and a blue heron.

Because she'd removed the remaining walls, the third floor was awash in light, exposing the years of wear on the scarred and scuffed floors that had yet to be sanded down, and the rough outer walls with their mis-matched, ancient wallpaper.

Tia didn't mind that her space wasn't finished. She had a vision, and she enjoyed each one of the steps to make that vision come alive.

The old kitchen appliances, in chipped green enamel, were also still there, until she decided just what she needed and wanted. Three floors was a long way to go if she had a sudden craving for pizza in the middle of the night, or if she was working late and needed a snack.

Her bed, a four poster carved from rosewood, sat beneath a three-part arched window in the center of the street-facing wall. The window was original to the house and one of the reasons Tia had chosen to make the third floor her bedroom.

The other, more important reason, was the view. As Tia circled the room she looked out over the Eastern Promenade and Casco Bay, Munjoy Hill, Back Cove, and the city of Portland. It was nothing short of spectacular.

She stopped by her drafting table, currently set in front of the windows that looked over Back Bay and her Bayside project. A rack beside the table held rolled copies of blueprints stuffed into large cardboard tubes. A copy of the blueprint for phase one lay spread out on the table. She looked at it for a long minute, then made up her mind.

"Come on, Dozer. We need to hit the woods." Dozer followed Tia into the corner where she kept her well used camping supplies. It only took her ten minutes to gather what she needed.

She called Miles and told him she had to leave town for a few days, then wrote Orion a quick note telling him to take the second floor suite and that she'd be back sometime Wednesday. She slapped the note on the wall beside the security alarm where he couldn't miss it.

Grabbing food for herself and Dozer plus his dishes, she tossed everything into her truck. A half hour later she was out of the city and headed west toward her favorite camping spot near the White Mountains, a mountain stream named Bull Branch.

Tia pushed away the thought that she was running. If she let herself think about what she was doing, she'd have to admit that Orion bothered her in ways that made her uncomfortable, and she definitely didn't want to go there.

Several hours after Tia's departure Jack Orion stood on her back deck and set his duffle with the clothes and personal items he needed at his feet. He'd taken his time packing, giving her the chance to get her house in order and get used to the idea of an unexpected house guest.

He rapped his fist on the back door, noting with satisfaction that it was solid, and waited for Dozer to bark. Nothing. Were they up on the third floor? He knocked harder, then stepped off the deck into the yard and checked the back windows. They were all dark. No one was at home.

Jack frowned. He hoped Tia hadn't been stupid and paid a visit to the build site by herself at night.

Pulling the key she'd given him, a key that unlocked either the front or back doors, he let himself into the dark house. Fortunately for him, the security panel was lit and he could see to disarm it.

Dammit, where was she? He'd expected her to be there waiting for him and had brought a bottle of wine to ease his way in. He found the fact that she wasn't waiting to greet him and show him her house irritating. And frustrating. Jack didn't do well with either emotion.

It took him a few minutes to find the panel of light switches hidden under one of Tia's jackets and then find the right switch for the kitchen. The woman must own fifty jackets. Just like at the front door, wall hooks held a variety of outerwear with boot trays beneath holding neatly lined up shoes and boots.

Jack stood where he was and looked about the space. Plain-fronted, Shaker-style cherry cabinets provided plenty of storage space in the roomy kitchen. Polished black granite counters provided ample work space for several people to work together.

Fresh herbs filled the deep sill of the window over the sink that looked out at the back yard, and some sort of red flowering plant he couldn't identify soaked up the sun from a west facing window. A deep blue enamel six-burner gas stove and matching refrigerator completed the kitchen area.

He wanted to see what else Tia had done with the house but he wanted her to personally show him. Poking around on his own felt like prying, and while he didn't have any problem prying into other people's business when necessary, he didn't want to do that to Tia.

Where the hell was she?

Jack turned to grab his duffle off the porch and saw the note next to the security panel. He'd missed it in the dark. Snatching it up, he read it and cursed. Camping! The woman had gone off camping–alone! Didn't she take the threats seriously? What if she had been followed? She could be murdered and her body hidden forever.

Cursing, Jack grabbed his duffle and carried it up to the second floor suite. He dumped it on the couch and glared at the space, in no mood to appreciate its comfort, or what a nice job Tia had done with the floors and the old plaster walls.

Where had she gone? He needed to know so he could go after her. He stomped up the back stairs to the third floor but found the door at the head of the stairs locked. For a brief moment he considered breaking it down, then just gave it a frustrated slam with his fist.

He headed back to the second floor suite end explored the space, made up the bed, and checked out the bathroom. A lovely mosaic of a mariner's compass done in soft blues and greens, a dusty red, and a muted gold anchored the center of the tiled floor. The woman was an artist, no doubt about it.

Just wait until she returned. He'd lay an earful on her, let her know just how stupid and dangerous her behavior was.

He heard a door close downstairs. Had he forgotten to lock it? Or had Tia given someone else a key to her house? God almighty, how many people had access here?

Thoroughly pissed off, Jack thundered down the stairs. He stopped at the bottom of the stairs when Dozer growled at him.

Jack ignored the relief flooding through his body, glared and pointed a finger at Tia. "We need to talk."

TIA BARELY GLANCED AT ORION. She tossed her pack on the floor and bent to untie her boots, all the while keeping a close watch on Dozer to see what he'd do. She didn't actually want him to bite Orion, but she was glad he was growling. Even though Dozer knew the man, he hadn't expected Orion's presence inside the house.

Jack sat on the bottom steps and watched Tia remove her boots. He was seething but knew he had to get a handle on himself. He didn't want Dozer to think of him as an enemy.

"Hello, Dozer," he said softly. "Remember me? It's Jack, good buddy." He presented the back of his hand for the dog to sniff.

Satisfied that Jack posed no threat, Dozer retreated to the dog bed Tia had set up for him and chewed on his rope.

"At least he growled at me."

Tia toed off her boots and picked up her pack. "I told you he was a good watch dog. There's no need for you to be here." She had yet to look directly at the man sitting on her back staircase. Eyes on his feet, she took a step toward him but he made no effort to move out of her way.

"I thought you were going camping."

"I changed my mind. Even though it wasn't my intention, it felt too much like running and I'll be damned if I'm going to let some jerk drive me out of my home." There. Let Orion figure out if she was referring to him or whoever was behind the threats.

"I never intended to drive you away," Jack said slowly. He pursed his lips and tilted his head. "Or were you running from whoever's been threatening you?"

The remark hit too close to Tia's own thoughts and elicited an angry scowl. "I *said* I wasn't running from you or whoever's behind the threats. I just felt the need to get out of the city for a couple days so I could clear my mind."

She turned away from the staircase and headed for the door that led past the half bath and laundry room and into the front entry and the other set of stairs.

"Wait, Tia." Jack stood and caught up with her. He placed a gentle hand on her shoulder. "I brought a bottle of wine with me. Why don't we share some and talk about the best way to work this out."

Tia hesitated. Did she want to drink wine with this man who disturbed her equilibrium? Self preservation said no, but a little piece of her wanted to know more about Jack Orion.

"All right. But only one glass."

"I promise, I'll try not to make a nuisance of myself while I'm here. I really am trying to help you."

"Fine. The wine glasses are in the cabinet to the right of the sink. I'm going to take my pack upstairs. I'll meet you on the back deck."

Tia took her time putting her camping gear away. She felt disgusted with herself for agreeing to a glass of wine. Orion was a player–she knew that and still she let herself succumb to his charm. Well, she would make sure everything between them remained all business while he was staying here.

Shored by her new determination to keep Jack Orion at arm's

length she headed down the back stairs and out onto the deck. Dozer sniffed around the yard, checking to see if any rabbits or squirrels had paid a visit while he'd been gone.

Tia took the offered glass of wine and sat in the Adirondack chair opposite Orion's. "Thank you." She took a sip and set the glass down on the low teak table that sat between the chairs. "I really don't see how you're being here is going to help."

So they were going to get right to it. No small talk or get to know each other better. Fine. Jack was ready. He looked at Tia over the rim of his glass as he sipped and took a moment to appreciate the silky feel of the Pinot Noir he had chosen. Notes of cherry and spice lingered in his mouth.

He twirled the glass stem between his thumb and fingers and watched the streetlight catch the deep red liquid, reminding him of precious rubies. He did enjoy fine wine and this one was meant to be savored.

"No answer to that? I guess you'll be on your way then."

Tia leaned forward to stand, but Jack's hand shot out. He pointed at her. "Sit. Please." He waited until she sat, scowling at him again.

"You're going to get worry lines between those pretty eyebrows of yours if you keep scowling at me like that," he said. "Here's the way I see it. The Bayside project is important to the city. You've come up with a lovely plan that will enhance not only the neighborhood, but will add beauty to the Portland skyline. Bayside will fill several needs—not only professional space but housing and shops, the kind of shops that make an area desirable.

"I'm happy to play a part in the development of Bayside," he continued. "This isn't a one woman show. Yes, you are the principal mover and shaker, but at this point others have something on the line as well if it all implodes."

"It isn't going to–"

Jack held up his hand to stop her. "I'm not finished. My point is that you *are* the principal mover and shaker. If anything happens to you Bayside will fall apart without your vision and guidance. If that happens I'll stand to lose a great deal of money. I don't like losing money. It's in my best interest to make sure nothing happens to you."

"I'm careful," Tia argued. "Nothing's going to happen to me. And I don't see how having you here will make any difference."

"The second threat was much more violent and explicit than the first one, Tia. The threats are escalating. Best case scenario, we figure out who's behind them and it all goes away. Until then I'm sleeping in your spare room in case anyone decides to try something at night–like burn you out."

Tia hadn't considered how violent the threats could get. She shuddered at the thought of all her hard work going up in flames. She picked up the wine and took a big gulp, missing Jack's wince as he watched her.

"Fine. You're here now. The third floor is mine and is off limits to you, whether I'm home or not. The suite on the second floor is all yours. Knock yourself out. If my parents decide to visit before we find the culprit you'll have to move out since that's their space."

"Fair enough. Nice job on that space, by the way. I especially like the tile work in the bathroom. The mariner's compass is a nice touch."

Tia pulled on her manners. "Thank you. It seemed fitting. There was a widow's walk on the roof when the house was built. I intend to replace it but it's low down on my list. I want to finish the inside first."

They talked about renovating houses for a while. Tia found Orion to be knowledgable and intelligent. She began to relax and even accepted a second glass of wine. Night had fallen and the neighborhood had grown quiet with the kids inside for the night. Dozer sat at her feet, snoozing with his head resting on his rope.

"So, what time do we run in the morning?" Jack asked.

Tia jerked upright. "What? What?" She pointed a finger at him. "I don't need you to run with me. Now that Dozer has his cast off I'll be taking him with me."

Jack lifted one shoulder in a lazy shrug. "I run every morning. We might as well run together. We don't have to talk. I'll respect your space."

Tia tried a few more excuses but Orion parried them all. She stood and looked down at him, his hair glowing in the shaft of light from the kitchen, a small smile on his impossibly handsome face.

"Six. I run at six. If you're up and ready you can run with us. I'm not waiting around for you."

Tia headed inside and up to the third floor. It wasn't until she was crawling under her comforter that she realized they hadn't talked about the other two companies who had bid on the Bayside project. Her prime suspects.

She punched her pillow. Damn that man. He had a way of throwing her off her stride that she didn't appreciate. Not one little bit.

CHAPTER 14

TIA'S LIFE fell into an uneasy rhythm with Orion. He met her at the back door every morning at six sharp, with his thick, sleep tousled hair and close-fitted tees, ready to run.

She refused to speak or even acknowledge him. She did her stretches up in her third floor space instead of on the back deck like she usually did, grabbed Dozer's leash and took off, stopping only for Dozer to take care of his bathroom needs.

To Orion's credit he never tried to talk to her in the morning. He simply held the door for her and Dozer, set the alarm, and matched her stride.

Dozer loved his morning runs. He raced her down the stairs and waited impatiently by the boots where his leash hung on a hook. After the first few attempts to cross in front of Tia to sniff something out and nearly getting run over in the process, he learned to run at her side.

After years of running alone Tia should have felt hemmed in, with Dozer on her right and Orion running on her left, but it felt natural, comfortable. Occasionally she'd break into a sprint, smiling until Orion caught up with her, then she'd wipe all

83

expression off her face. It wouldn't do to let the man know she was actually beginning to enjoy his company.

She noticed more women running early and figured the word had gotten out that Jack Orion could be found running the Eastern Promenade at six in the morning. The women showed up in designer leggings and fancy bras, in full makeup and blown dry hair. They tried everything they could to catch his eye, even going so far as to fake-stumble into him.

He simply smiled and kept on running after setting the stumbler to rights. But not before one woman had pressed her body up against his and licked his arm.

Tia began to feel a little sorry for Orion. He was being subjected to improper sexual advances, the same way women had always suffered. Then she remembered the photos of Orion, always with a different woman, and her sympathy vanished.

Evenings were a little tougher for Tia to ignore. She enjoyed cooking. She always had. Even as a young girl she'd join her mother and aunts in the big family kitchen and ask to help. Cooking relaxed her and helped her work through any frustrations or problems the day might have held. It was a safe outlet for her, one that paid dividends because she loved to eat good food and didn't care much for restaurants.

Much to her surprise, at the beginning of the second week of Orion's stay at her house, he announced that he was making dinner.

She leaned against the island in her faded sweat pants and even more faded Moody Blues tee shirt, her hair wet from her shower, and accepted the glass of sauvignon blanc Orion handed her while she watched him work.

He wore a similar outfit, although his tee shirt stretched across his impressive chest while Tia's was intentionally loose and revealed nothing. She knew she was deficient in the breast department–her brothers had often teased her about it–and she saw no reason to advertise the fact.

Blues music played quietly in the background. Dozer lay on his bed, gnawing on his rope while keeping a close eye on the food preparation in case something fell on the floor.

Soon the kitchen was filled with the fragrance of warmed virgin olive oil and garlic. Orion added capers and anchovies, fried some boneless chicken thighs in the mixture and stuck them in the oven to finish cooking. Tia's mouth watered as she watched him whip together a salad, squeeze lemon juice on the finished chicken and carry it all to the table.

"Where'd you learn to cook like this?" she asked. The chicken was delicious and she made a little hum in her throat as she took another bite.

"Like it?" Jack smiled. He rarely showed off his culinary skills to a woman because it always got them thinking about marriage, a condition he had no interest in. Women were for fun and good times until he grew bored with them, not for anything permanent. He only brought women to his loft for sex, and then he got rid of them as politely and quickly as possible.

But he had begun to feel guilty about eating the meals Tia prepared for them, especially since he had essentially forced her to take him in–an unwanted guest in her home.

"Mostly I taught myself," he admitted. "I like to eat good food and I don't always feel like going out to a restaurant. The way I saw it I didn't have much choice. Learn to cook or starve. Turns out I really enjoy it."

Tia raised an eyebrow. This was the most honest, personal thing Orion had shared with her since she'd met him. She raised her wine glass in a toast. "My compliments to the chef. This is delicious. I'm glad I watched you make it so I can replicate the recipe after you're gone."

They finished the meal in a companionable silence. Since

Orion cooked, Tia handled clean up and then took Dozer outside for his last pee of the evening.

Jack left her to it. He sprawled in one of the leather chairs in his sitting room with a book and listened for her steps on the stairs and overhead as she got ready for bed. What had he gotten himself into?

It had started as a game. Get Tia into bed. That's all he he'd wanted. Learning about the slashed tires and another threat against her on the day of the cookout with her friend Cass's family had seemed like a gift. He'd pounced on the chance to insert himself into Tia's life without thinking it through.

He tossed the book on the couch, disgusted with himself. Now he was doing the one thing he had promised himself he'd never get roped into–he was living with a woman. What had he been thinking? He hadn't, that was the problem. He had only been thinking about making the conquest.

Idiot.

And tonight. Tonight he had wanted to make dinner for her. He saw how hard Tia worked. How she faced a dirty construction site day after day, how she came home bone weary yet glowing because her vision was taking shape.

And she was so gentle and patient and loving with the stray, Dozer. The pup obviously adored her. And Cass, her three boys, and her husband Leonard were the same way. Tia had a very small, tight circle, but it was solid. There wasn't a phony cell in her body.

He hadn't expected that. He hadn't expected the soft center under the tough shell that Tia presented to the world.

Dammit, he needed to get out of there before he completely lost his mind. Fortunately he knew just the thing to break the spell Tia was weaving around him. He had a date with Tamara Friday night. Some fund raiser at the Portland Museum of Art that he had agreed to escort her to months ago.

The beautiful Tamara who could turn any man's head and looked good on his arm. He'd seen the photos of them in the Portland paper. They made a splash wherever they went.

Tamara liked expensive things. He'd take her to Haggerty's—the new hot spot in Portland's Old Port district for dinner before the fund raiser. Tamara also liked to be seen at all the right places.

He knew she'd be dressed to the nines in a new designer gown since she never wore the same thing twice, her signature diamonds on her ears and around her neck and wrist, her pale blonde hair swept up, not a hair out of place. The perfect woman, and every man envied him when he had her on his arm.

It hardly mattered that she carried that cool reserve into his bed.

Jack frowned. Tamara had dropped a few subtle hints their last two dates. Hints that she'd be agreeable to making things more permanent between them. That her father, Randolf Albrecht, would be agreeable to as well. Randolf and his mega-millions. An alliance of power and money. A man could do worse.

He heard Tia walk across the ceiling toward where he imagined her bed to be. He'd been in her house more than a week and had yet to see her space on the third floor.

Tia, who was not Tamara.

Tia, with her wild, black curls and intelligent eyes the color of green moss, her long lean, athletic body and incredible legs. And those calloused hands. Why did he find her hands so endearing?

Tia, who would bring her passion for life to his bed. The opposite of Tamara.

He really needed to get out of there. No more wasting time trying to get Tia into bed. He needed to focus on her problem and get back to his perfect life.

An image flashed into his mind of that athletic body held

naked against his own. With a groan, Jack decided he'd better put himself to bed.

Tomorrow after their run he'd tackle the problem of who was making threats against Tia. Once that was solved he could leave.

Unfortunately he was afraid it might already be too late. While he'd been focused on bedding her, Artemis Smith had gotten under his skin.

CHAPTER 15

"Cass, I'm running a little late. I should be there in twenty or thirty minutes. I'll call if I'm going to be any later. I'll bring wine."

Tia shut off her phone and tossed it back into her canvas pack. What a day it had been. The end of the work week for her crew and she swore everyone's brains had taken the day off.

Marty, usually so level-headed, had rolled the loader tractor when he tried to move an over-full load of sand across a hill. Fortunately for them both, Tia insisted on the men strapping in when they ran the equipment and each piece had rollover protection bars to protect the operator from being crushed.

Still, it had given everyone a scare and taken hours to set right. Marty had been too shaken to finish the task and Tia had sent him home to his wife after a trip to the emergency room to get checked out. Most of the heavy equipment operators were overweight and Marty was no exception. They didn't exercise and they sat on their machines all day. Tia worried about their hearts and their blood pressure but they ignored her hints about exercise and eating right.

After Marty's incident things just sort of cascaded from there. Andrew wasn't paying attention when the crane operator placed a concrete form and it landed on his foot. Another trip to the emergency room for x-rays. Andrew had a broken foot (surprise) and would be out of work for the next month at least. He needed to be replaced and Tia added it to her growing to-do list.

Some of the concrete forms for the first story walls had been the wrong size. More time wasted calling the company who rented them and getting the right ones delivered and the wrong ones hauled off. Then the company owner insisted he had to charge her for the wrong ones even though the mistake had been his fault, not hers.

Tia had bearded the idiot in his office with the paperwork, showed him the error of his ways, and refused to leave until she saw the charges reversed. Idiot. Some days they seemed to be the only ones populating the world.

She had never been so happy to see a Friday herald the start of a weekend. She preferred to schedule six work-day weeks but after today she realized the men needed a break. Their brains were turning to mush. There were a few grumblings about the lost overtime pay but nothing serious. They knew they needed a rest.

Tia had waved everyone off and was waiting for the night watchman to arrive. Locking the gate was Miles's job but he had begged off tonight. He had a hot date and wanted time to get ready. Tia grinned. Miles was worse than a woman, needing time to primp for the opposite sex. She couldn't imagine Orion doing that—a quick shower and shave and toss on his clothes and he'd be ready. Ready and looking great.

And why had she thought of Orion?

She shook her head. It was a good thing she'd made plans to have dinner with Cass's family tonight. She was beginning to look forward to seeing Orion after the work day and having someone to discuss the day with. It surprised her to discover that she liked having someone to cook for and share a meal with. Especially someone as intelligent and interesting as Jack Orion.

Things were growing a little too cozy with Orion for her taste. She needed him to leave. He had been deflecting her inquiries into who might be behind the threats, but she'd force the issue when she saw him tonight.

"Come on, Dozer, let's wander the site while we wait." She reached down and tugged gently on Dozer's ears. He smiled his doggy smile and licked her arm. "Yeah, you're all I need, aren't you boy?"

Tia closed the gate but left it unlocked for the night watchman, then took off along the fence with Dozer at her side, checking for any sign of tampering. She knew the watchman would patrol the perimeter several times through the night, but it never hurt to check things for herself.

Traffic noises from Forest Avenue—workers escaping the city after a long work week and heading home to their suburban havens—sounded loud in the now quiet site. Horns blared as someone wasn't fast enough responding to a green light.

Seagulls called over the bay that still held mackerel for recreational fishermen. The colorful triangular sails of windsurfers enjoying the beautiful early evening caught her eye. Portland offered plenty of recreational opportunities for those stuck in the city. It was one of the things she loved about living there.

She stopped for a moment to watch a pair of windsurfers race each other across the bay and laughed when the woman edged out her male friend and raised her fist in triumph.

Tia checked her sturdy, much-abused watch. The night guard was running late. Dammit. She sighed. She should have expected this after the day she'd had. She continued along the fence line toward the rear of the site. After the night of the tire slashings she had instructed the men to leave the heavy equipment spread out over the site and toward the front. She couldn't afford to replace any more tires.

She peered between a tall pile of mis-sized concrete forms that the men had set out of the way until the company could pick them up, and the fence. It was a perfect spot to cut through without anyone noticing.

Almost as if she'd conjured them out of the air, she spotted a pair of red-handled bolt cutters lying just inside the fence, halfway down the narrow space. What were they doing there?

She looked outside the fence but didn't see anyone hanging around. The space was almost too narrow for even her slim frame, but she squeezed in. She heard Dozer bark once behind her and called to him but there was no response from the pup.

"Dozer? Where are you, boy? Is this too tight and scary? I'll meet you out the other side in a minute. I'm almost there." She pushed against the flexible chain link fence to create more space and pushed forward. It was tighter than she expected and her shoulders were squeezed, the rough edges of the forms grabbing her shirt and scratching her bare arm. No wonder the dog hadn't wanted to follow her.

"Dozer!" Tia whistled, the special two-tone whistle that she used especially for him. "Here, boy!" She popped out the far side of the gap and rubbed her beat-up arm. Movement above her shoulder caught her eye. How had Dozer climbed the pile of forms?

Something heavy landed on top of her, knocking her to the ground. She gasped and tried to roll but she was pinned. Her wrists were pulled behind her back and zip-tied together. Before she could twist around to see her assailant a large bag was thrown over her head, effectively blinding her.

Tia kicked, trying to catch the assailant's legs but he sat on them and used another zip-tie to immobilize her. The bag was pulled down over her feet, completely enclosing her.

Where was her night watchman? Would he show up in time to catch this guy before he kidnapped her? Tia yelled as loud as she could, hoping someone would hear her.

"Bitch. You should have backed off. Now you pay." The voice was a deep and raspy whisper. An *angry* whisper. Something big and meaty slammed into Tia's cheek. Pain exploded in her face and sparks of light danced in front of her eyes. The bag felt like it was suffocating her. What was he doing?

Dazed from the blow, it took her a minute to recognize the sound of duct tape. He was duct-taping her head so she wouldn't be able to make a sound.

The rough fabric of the canvas bag pressed against her face. Tears sprang to her eyes when he pressed on her shattered cheek. He wrapped several strips around her arms, legs, and head, effectively immobilizing her. Surely the watchman would stop this man, whoever he was, from carrying her out of the site?

She heard a distant noise, the clang of metal, and a vehicle. Her night watchman had arrived.

"Shit." The man shoved her back in between the pile of forms and the fence and threw something on top of her. Then all was silent.

Tia lay still for several minutes, waiting to see if he would return. Her cheek throbbed painfully.

Where was Dozer? Had the man hurt her pup? At least she could breath. The duct tape covered her mouth area and throat, but he hadn't had time to tape her entire head. If he had, she would be suffocating.

Had that been the assailant's intention? To kill her? Maybe he had planned to throw her in the bay where she would have drowned. The thought made gooseflesh rise on her skin and filled her with panic.

The rough canvas abraded her skin and smelled musty and salty. An old sail bag? That was the only canvas style bag she could think of that would be long enough to cover her entire body.

She tried wiggling but was jammed tight.

Something wiggled on top of her and she heard heavy breathing. He was still there, lying on top of her to hide from the night watchman.

Her heart raced and she began to hyperventilate.

After several long minutes Tia realized the weight lying on top of her was too light to be a man. She forced herself to slow her breathing. Then she heard a small whine and realized her assailant had tossed Dozer on top of her. Was her dog bagged up as well?

There was nothing she could do but wait for the watchman to find them. Hopefully he would be thorough enough to check the fence behind the pile of forms. If he didn't . . . she didn't want to think about it. They wouldn't be found until at least Monday afternoon when the form rental company removed the pile of wrong-sized forms.

Her cheek throbbed. A hard, sharp corner was jammed into her hip. Her hands were going numb from the zip-ties. She tried to push against the ties and only succeeded in digging them into her wrists. She felt blood and stopped. It was futile to try. Everyone knew that zip-ties were unbreakable. Even law enforcement used them.

Time dragged on. The sound of traffic died. The light behind the bag faded. She heard the night watchman walk by the pile of forms but he didn't come close enough for her to get his attention.

She was going to fire his ass. First thing, when she was freed. Dozer whined, but she couldn't speak to reassure him. She felt the temperature drop–spring nights in Maine could still get pretty cool–and she shivered.

No one was going to find her until Monday.

CHAPTER 16

THE FUND RAISER at the Portland Art museum was a rousing success, judging by all the money people Jack had talked with so far that evening. It was nearly midnight and over half the original crowd still hung in there.

The museum had unveiled a new collection of thirteen Winslow Homer paintings recently donated by another museum as the high point of the gathering and everyone seemed in a giving mood. He had certainly pledged his share. He appreciated good art and was partial to Maine artists.

Jack snagged another shrimp cracker, but passed on the champagne offered by a tired looking waitress in a crisp black skirt and white blouse. He tried to sneak a peek at his watch, but Tamara caught him and gave a slight shake of her head.

They had been working the room for the last three hours, after a disappointing meal at Haggerty's. Disappointing to Jack anyway, although Tamara had seemed happy to enjoy a prime table in the crowded restaurant. She rarely did more than pick at her food no matter how good it was, so she probably hadn't noticed how bland the meal had been.

Almost the opposite of Tia's style. Tia truly enjoyed food and ate with a hearty relish that was a pleasure to see and a compliment to the cook, even when she had done the cooking. She would have scoffed at Haggerty's.

Jack brought his attention back to the party. Tamara was looking for investors interested in her father's newest line of brew, and Jack had taken advantage of the evening to add to his pool of possible investors because that was what he did–lined potential investors up with projects that suited their investing philosophy.

Jack smiled a fake smile at the uber boring couple he and Tamara were currently making light chitchat with. The man, an older, silver-haired investment banker, had a young, beautiful wife on his arm. The proverbial trophy wife.

His first wife probably put him through school and raised his children, kept his house and threw parties to help his career, and then was repaid for her efforts by being ousted for a younger, fresher model. A younger, fresher model who was definitely trying to let Jack know she was interested in him.

Why was he feeling so jaded tonight? He usually loved schmoozing, and on any other night the wife would have entertained him instead of disgusting him.

Tamara smiled up at him and tucked her hand possessively under his arm. She looked stunning in her pale blue sheath and diamonds, not a hair out of place.

The Ice Princess.

The label, while accurate, startled him and made Jack feel guilty. The urge for some fresh air washed over him. He patted Tamara's hand and removed it. "I need to find the little boy's room. I'll be right back."

She smiled, her eyes already searching the room for her next target. Had she always acted like this when they were out together? Her smile turned to a puzzled frown and he realized he was frowning at her.

"Jack, darling, are you all right? Was it something you ate?" Concern showed in Tamara's pale blue eyes. Eyes that matched the shade of her sheath exactly. Such a cold color.

He wondered who in Daddy's empire had been tasked with the job of finding fabric in that exact shade of blue. Most likely she had the fabric dyed to her specifications. Come to think of it she wore that color a lot.

Jesus, he needed an attitude check. He had looked forward to this evening's fund raiser with Tamara, knowing it would help him break away from the cozy routine he was falling into with Tia. Remind him of where he belonged.

He had enjoyed himself tonight, right up until the moment they'd arrived at the restaurant–and then he'd wanted nothing more than to be cooking Tia dinner and sharing a glass of good wine while talking over the day with her. He had discovered that Tia was a good listener; and smart, funny, and passionate when she talked about her crew and the Bayside project.

She entertained him and she was easy to be with. Almost the opposite of Tamara in every way. He could not picture Tamara dressed in old sweats and a faded rock tee. She'd rather go naked than be seen in what she would call "rags".

Jack gave himself a mental shake. He wasn't being fair to Tamara. She was a lovely woman. In fact she was everything he wanted in a woman. Educated, poised, upper crust. So why was he feeling so disgruntled?

The first seed of discontent this evening had come when he had met Tamara at her hotel and she had handed him her overnight bag to place in the trunk of his new Mercedes roadster. She'd done it without asking, assuming Jack would want to take her back to his loft after the party. He always had, so why would tonight be any different?

Only tonight *was* different. He wasn't going back to his loft tonight because he was living at Tia's. He wished he had said something right when Tamara handed him her bag, but he had kept quiet, and now it loomed over him, that he had to tell Tamara he was sleeping at another woman's house.

She wouldn't be pleased, and there was no telling what Tamara would do if she wasn't pleased. Jack had a feeling very few people crossed Tamara Albrecht.

"Darling? What's wrong?"

Jack realized he hadn't moved after excusing himself to use the bathroom. The banker looked uncomfortable. His wife used the tip of her tongue to lick her lower lip and winked at him. Tamara looked genuinely concerned.

"I'm fine. I'll be back in a minute." He turned and pushed his way through the crush of people until he reached the hall where the rest rooms were located, but didn't stop. He kept going until he stood outside, under one of the museum's front arches, and took several deep breaths of cooler air.

The traffic on Congress Street was steady, and small knots of people had gathered on the large brick sidewalk that fronted the museum almost like an old-time square. A diesel truck rattled by, spewing noxious fumes.

Before Jack could turn to head back inside to Tamara, he felt his phone vibrate in his pocket. He pulled it out to see if Tia was calling, but it was Cassidy Reali.

Jack frowned. Why would Tia's friend be calling him at this late hour?

"Hello?"

"Jack! It's Cass. I'm trying to get a hold of Tia. She isn't answering her phone. Is she there?"

Something dark and foreboding twisted in Jack's gut. "I'm not at the house, Cass. I'm at the museum's annual fund raiser. I'm sure she must be in bed by now."

"I don't think so. We were supposed to get together for dinner tonight but I had an emergency show up at the clinic. I called to let her know that I'd be held up but Len and the boys would be waiting for her, but she never answered her phone then either. It keeps going to voice mail."

"Maybe she forgot and turned it off. She does that sometimes." Much to his irritation.

"No." Cass sounded exasperated. "Jack, listen to me. Tia had called me not five minutes earlier to say she was picking up the wine and would be here in twenty minutes. *She never got here.* Jack, I'm really worried. What if that lunatic who's been threatening her got to her? Would you–would you mind leaving the party and swinging by the house? Just to make sure she's okay? She'll kill me for this, but–"

Jack didn't wait for her to finish. "I need to tell someone I'm leaving, then I'll head straight to Tia's. I'll call you from there."

"I'll wait up. Don't forget to call."

"I won't. I promise." He slipped his phone back into his pocket and pushed back inside the museum, nearly clipping a woman on his way through the door.

He told Tamara that he had a problem client he had to deal with and it couldn't wait, shoved some cab money at her, and ran out. She wasn't at all happy, and he had her overnight bag in his car, probably filled with essentials that she needed, but it couldn't be helped. He'd make it up to her somehow.

Jack raced to Tia's as fast as he could safely drive. The windows were all dark. He let himself inside and disengaged the alarm. Other than the hum of the refrigerator, the house was silent.

He checked the dishwasher and sink rack but saw no sign that Tia had made herself a meal. Maybe she grabbed something on the way home since he had told her he was going out that evening.

Jack took the steps to the third floor two at a time. He pounded on her door and called Tia's name. She didn't answer and Dozer didn't bark at him. They weren't there. He knew they weren't there but he had to make sure that nobody had gotten to her inside the house.

He slammed his shoulder into the door and bounced off. The damn thing was solid oak. He stepped back and gave it a vicious kick near the handle. It took three more before the door finally popped open.

Jack raced into the room and instantly saw that it was empty. He didn't waste any more time looking in the house. Tia wasn't there.

He pulled out his phone as he ran back to his car and dialed Cass. "She's not there. Where was she when she called you?"

"Still at the site. Miles had a date and left early so she was waiting for the night watchman. She said he'd be there any minute. My emergency showed up about ten minutes later and I tried to call her back but she didn't answer. What do we do?"

They both knew that the police wouldn't let them file a missing persons report until after twenty four hours had passed. Jack had no intention of sitting around and waiting.

"I'll head to the site and take a look around."

"Call me when you find her. I won't be able to sleep until I know she's safe."

Neither would Jack. "I'll call as soon as I know something."

CHAPTER 17

JACK MADE it to the Bayside building site in under five minutes. He parked the roadster in front of the gate and climbed out. The site had three night security lights, one in front and each side. The back of the site was shrouded in shadows.

He tried the gate but it was locked. Grabbing onto the fence, he did a visual sweep of the site. It looked quiet. The heavy equipment was scattered about, all toward the front lighted area.

An older dark blue RAV sat parked just inside the gate, empty. Jack looked for the night watchman and caught movement off to the far right perimeter. The watchman made the corner and headed his way. He hesitated when he saw Jack standing at the gate, then approached slowly.

When he came to a stop in front of the gate Jack could see the guy was young and beefy, more fat than muscle. Was this the best Tia could do? The guy looked like a cream puff. He couldn't scare off a group of twelve year olds.

"This is private property," the watchman said. "You'll have to leave or I'll call the police. *Now.* You have to leave now." His voice cracked from nerves. He reached into his pocket and Jack wondered if he carried a gun, but he pulled out a phone. "I'm calling the cops."

"Go ahead. I'd love to get them here. I'm Jack Orion, Tia Smith's partner. I'm looking for her. She missed an appointment earlier this evening and seems to be missing. Is anyone else here?"

Jack knew he presented an odd picture, appearing at the gate in the middle of the night still dressed in his tuxedo.

"No. I'm alone." The watchman shook his head. "The boss lady ain't here. Her truck's here, but I ain't seen no one since I arrived."

"Tia's truck is here?" The dark ball of apprehension in Jack's gut grew. "She wouldn't leave her truck here. She was supposed to meet a friend as soon as you showed up. You have to let me in. I need to see for myself."

The guard hesitated, obviously not sure if Jack could be trusted.

"Oh for crying out loud." Dress shoes were not made for scaling chainlink fences, but somehow Jack made it up and over. He landed on the ground next to the guard, who clearly wasn't sure what to do.

"What time did you get here?" Jack asked him.

The guard mumbled something.

"What?" Jack stepped closer and gave him the hard stare that made a lot of men quake in their shoes. Jack was a big guy, and he knew how to use his size to intimidate.

"I said I was thirty minutes late, okay? I had a flat tire when I left for work and I had to change it."

"And Tia was here when you arrived?"

"Nobody was here. That's what I've been telling you. The gate was unlocked, so I drove in and locked it. I've been making my rounds like Mr. Angsley told me to do. I ain't done nothing wrong."

And you probably haven't done much right. Why hadn't Tia hired a better qualified guard? "Show me where Tia's truck is parked."

"Over there. Behind the dozer." The guard pointed. "I was just over there. I'm telling you, nobody's here but me."

"You said that already. Wait here" He looked at the kid who was so obviously unqualified to be a night guard. "I changed my mind. Come with me. We're going to search the equipment."

"Why? I told you I'm the only one here."

Jack headed for the dozer. "Because, Mr. Night Watchman, someone has threatened Tia's life twice now. That's why you were hired."

The guard's face paled and took on a sickly green tone under the halogen lights. "Geez, no one told me the job could be dangerous. They shoulda told me."

Jack was going to wring Tia's neck for not being honest with the guard. He spotted her truck behind the dozer and changed course for it. The cab was unlocked. He climbed in and made a quick, cursory search but didn't find the truck keys or that ratty canvas pack she always carried. She must have it with her, which meant she had her phone.

And that meant that something or someone was keeping her from answering it.

His fear grew into something more solid and threatening.

"That's private property," the guard pointed out. "You probably shouldn't be doing that."

Jack climbed out of the truck and headed for the dozer while the guard struggled to keep up. A quick check of the dozer's cab and behind the blade revealed nothing.

He searched each piece of equipment, then stood in the middle of the site with his hands on his hips. The guard panted beside him, winded from trying to keep pace with Jack's long strides as he criss-crossed the site.

"You really think she's here somewhere?" the guard asked.

"Yes." The alternative was too horrible for Jack to consider. If Tia had been kidnapped they might never find her.

"Where are the cameras?"

"I don't think they're hooked up yet. Mr. Angsley said something about maybe by next week."

Jack was going to have a serious talk with Tia's foreman tomorrow.

"And you've walked the perimeter of the fence since you've been here."

The guard nodded, pleased that he hadn't failed to do his job. "Yup. Twice. Except where all the stuff is piled up, of course. I just skirted around that stuff cause it's in the way."

Jack made a frustrated sound in his throat. "Give me your flashlight."

"It needs a new battery. I used the light on my phone. See?" He held up his cell phone and waved the light in a circle around them. "Works great, don't it? I'll get batteries tomorrow."

He wouldn't have a job tomorrow if Jack had anything to say about it.

"Wait here, or go back to your car. I'm going to search the back of the lot."

The guard looked worried. "You really think something happened to her, don't you?"

Jack didn't reply. He couldn't. As long as he didn't put his fear into words he could keep it contained.

"I'm coming with you. I'll help you search."

"Fine. We'll stick together. That way I know every spot has been checked."

They headed for the back left corner of the lot, checking along the fence, under tarp-covered stacks of framing lumber, and around every pile of dirt.

What if Tia had been buried in one of the dirt piles? Jack ruthlessly pushed the thought away. He couldn't face the possibility that they might be searching for a body. Tia was alive. He needed to stay focused on that.

His heart leaped into his throat when he spotted Dozer's rope toy lying in the dirt at the base of a pile of concrete forms. He picked it up and shook off the dirt. Dozer would never leave his beloved rope behind. He carried it with him everywhere.

"What's that?" asked the guard.

"A dog toy. They were here." Jack began to search around the base of the pile of forms, looking for what, he couldn't say. A clue. Something. Anything.

He had almost reached the fence on the third side of the pile when his foot struck something soft and lumpy. He dropped to his knees and pulled out Tia's canvas bag. It had been stuffed partially under the forms.

"Is that hers too?"

"Yes." Jack stepped to the fence. He had assumed the forms had been stacked right up against the fence, but now that he stood next to it, he could feel a narrow space with his hands. He pulled out his cell phone and flashed the light behind the pile. The light caught the dingy gray of an old sail bag.

Two bags. Two bags holding bodies. One small and one Tia-sized. Two bags that showed no signs of life.

His heart sank. At the same time his anger grew. Anger at himself for not taking better care of Tia, and anger at whoever had killed her. Jack made a silent promise to find Tia's killer and make him pay in as painful a way as he could devise.

He snapped a photo for the police, knowing they wouldn't be happy about him messing with a crime scene, then put his cell phone away. Grabbing the end of the smaller bag, he pulled it toward him. He hesitated a moment before opening it, not wanting to see the dead face of the puppy that Tia had rescued and loved so much.

When he realized Dozer was still alive he shouted to the

guard to call an ambulance and go unlock the gate for it. He set Dozer gently aside and reached back in to pull the larger sail bag toward him, wincing as it was squeezed between the fence and the immovable pile.

Jack stopped pulling and tried to crawl into the narrow space but he was too large. "I'm sorry sweetheart, this is probably going to hurt but it's the only way to get you out. You can bitch at me later, okay?"

Tia didn't answer. Panicked, Jack flashed his phone light again and saw the strips of duct tape around the bag. She couldn't answer even if she wanted to. He wished she would move, anything to let him know that she was still alive.

The sound of an approaching siren pierced the night.

"The cavalry is on the way, Tia. You hang in there, you here me? I'll have you out of there in a minute. This will hurt but you're tough. You're the toughest woman I know."

While he talked he continued to slide the bag toward him. By the time the ambulance drove through the gate he had photographed the bag, removed the tape, and had pulled the bag down to Tia's feet. He winced when he saw her bloodied wrists and swollen, bruised face and took several more photos.

"I'll kill whoever did this to you," he said as he cut the ties holding her wrists and ankles.

"We'll take it from here, sir." An EMT tapped Jack on the shoulder. He had been so focused on Tia he hadn't heard the ambulance drive up. The EMTs placed Tia on a rolling stretcher and drove off with its siren wailing and Jack running across the site after it.

"We found her." The guard sounded proud and happy. Jack started to growl at him but realized the kid wasn't to blame for any of what had happened.

"Yeah, we found her. Good job getting the ambulance back there."

The guard beamed at him. "Too bad they couldn't take the dog too," he said.

Oh crap. Dozer. Jack drove his car to the back of the site and carefully lifted the unconscious pup onto the leather passenger seat.

"Lock the gates behind me," he told the guard on his way back out.

"Yes, sir. You can trust me, sir."

Yeah, he probably could. The guard had learned several valuable lessons tonight and would be a better watchman for them.

CHAPTER 18

JACK RANG the bell to Cassidy's vet clinic and waited. He had seen the light on deep in the house, where he knew her kitchen was, and figured she was still awake. Sure enough, she pulled the door open a few short minutes later.

"Jack! Why didn't you call?" Cass tightened the belt of her robe around her waist and scowled at him.

"I was busy. Dozer needs your help."

"Dozer? Where is he? Where's Tia?"

"Dozer's in my car. I was afraid to move him again. Tia's at the hospital. I'm heading there as soon as I can tell her that Dozer is okay."

"Right."

He had to admire the way Cass flipped into competent veterinarian mode. She followed him out to the car and ran her hands gently over Dozer's body.

"I don't feel anything to alarm me. It looks as if he's been tranqed."

"Tranqed?"

"Tranquilizer. Bring him inside for me so I can check his vital signs."

"He's certainly grown since the last time I carried him in here," he remarked as he laid Dozer on the exam table.

"Yeah. He's happy, well cared for, and much loved." Cass listened to Dozer's heartbeat and checked his eyes and mouth. "Tia has always had a way with animals," she continued. It's like she can climb inside their heads and see what they're thinking and feeling. I've even brought her in to consult for me a few times when I've had a patient who should be responding to treatment but wasn't."

Cass eyed Jack's tuxedo. He had ripped one sleeve climbing the fence and there were dirt patches on the knees of his pants. "Nice outfit. You were at a fund raiser when I called?"

"For the museum. I go every year."

"Uh-huh. And I assume you brought a date?"

Jack narrowed his eyes. "What are you getting at Cass? Of course I brought a date. It's not like Tia and I are a couple. I'm just staying at her place to protect her from the nutcase who's been threatening her." Too late, he saw the glint in Cass's eyes.

"And how's that working out for Tia?" she asked softly.

She wasn't being mean. Jack didn't think there was a mean bone in Cass's small body. But she sure knew how to lay a "I'm disappointed in you" on a man without saying the words. No wonder her boys adored and obeyed her.

He huffed out a big breath and ran his hand through his hair. "Not too well, I have to admit. I promise you I'll do a better job than I did tonight. No more dates until I move out of Tia's."

Tamara wouldn't be happy about that, but it couldn't be helped. Someone had nearly succeeded in killing Tia tonight. He had a feeling her assailant had been interrupted by the guard and had stuffed Tia and Dozer behind the pile of forms instead of taking them somewhere else to finish the job.

It still could have turned out badly for them. If he hadn't

found them tonight Tia and Dozer wouldn't have been discovered until Monday after the pile had been moved.

"I promise you, Cass." Jack repeated. "Nothing like this will happen again."

"Good. Now why don't you leave Dozer with me tonight so I can keep an eye on him in case there's any after effects from the tranq? The boys have the day off from school tomorrow and they'll be thrilled to have a playmate. Call me from the hospital after you've checked on Tia. I'm going to bed now, but I'll check my messages as soon as I get up."

Jack wasted no time driving into the Maine Medical Center and tracking Tia down. She'd already been treated in emergency and was set up in a double room.

This time of night the corridor lights were somewhat dimmed and the rooms were dark.

He could hear various machines beeping and whooshing, the quiet murmur of the night nurses at the nurse's station, the rumble of the night janitor's cart as he pushed it slowly down the corridor, emptying waste baskets as he went. The place smelled of disinfectant and unclean bodies. No one ever got a decent shower in a hospital.

The elevator dinged and a woman dressed in green scrubs came hurrying out and disappeared inside one of the rooms. Jack focused on the room numbers. He hated hospitals, but then, everyone hated hospitals. All the suffering, and the reminder of just how frail the human body really is, was hard to face.

He found Tia's room and entered without knocking. He didn't want to wake her or the unknown roommate if they were asleep.

Tia had the bed nearest the door. Jack barely suppressed a gasp when he saw her. The left side of her face was swollen and bruised, and bruises and scrapes ran down both arms, which laid outside the thin white blanket.

He had to take several deep, calming breaths before he could bring himself to sit in the chair beside her bed. An IV ran out of the back of her right hand, but that was the only thing she was hooked up to.

That had to be a good thing, he told himself. If she was seriously injured surely there would be more equipment?

Jack started to take her hand but didn't want to disturb the IV. Her arms looked too bruised to touch. Now that he was sitting closer he could see more bruises peeking out of the neck of her hospital gown. Was she bruised all over? When he caught the man who'd hurt her he was going to leave twice as many bruises—and make sure the man knew why he was getting each one.

"Dozer?"

The whisper startled Jack. He leaned close to her. "Tia? Are you awake?"

Tia licked her lips but her eyes remained closed. "Gave me drugs. For pain. My dog?"

"Dozer's fine. I brought him to Cass. She thinks he was drugged. She'll keep him tonight and we'll pick him up on our way home tomorrow."

Tia started to smile and winced instead. "Thank you." She moved her head slightly. "Stupid. I was . . . stupid."

Damn he wanted to hold her hand, wanted to connect with her, but he was afraid to touch that bruised skin.

"No. You weren't stupid. The guard should have been there but he had a flat tire and was late. And now that I'm saying that out loud I suspect that he had been given a deliberate flat so he *would* be late. Dammit. I need to call the cops and file a report. Someone might have seen something."

"Doubt . . . ful. I'm sorry."

Jack scowled at Tia. "What are you sorry for? You didn't do anything wrong."

"Ruined your date."

"I was getting bored anyway. I would have had more fun arguing with you over wine and a home-cooked meal." And damn, that was the truth.

Tia huffed what he thought was a laugh and he smiled. "How did you know it was me, anyway? I didn't speak and you haven't opened your eyes."

"Smell."

"I smell?" Jack didn't know if he should feel insulted or if Tia was teasing him.

"You smell . . . clean. Like soap and man. Like my brothers, only better. I need to sleep."

"Right. I should leave. I had to bully my way past the nurses. I'll be back in the morning."

Jack stood and moved to the door, but didn't leave. He watched Tia for several more minutes while she slept, reluctant to leave her unguarded. Her curls lay dark and silky against the pillow, tempting him to touch them, but he was afraid of waking her again.

On the drive home he thought about how the attack on Tia had been orchestrated. Miles had left early for a date. The night watchman had left his apartment to go to work and found a flat which delayed him by twenty to thirty minutes. Tia had left the gate unlocked for the guard, expecting him to arrive any minute, and then took a final look around the site while she waited.

He made a mental note to track down Miles and speak with him. How did the assailant know that Tia would be alone at the site at that time?

Jack continued to gnaw on the timing issue until he reached his loft apartment. He needed to change out of his tux and switch vehicles before he headed to Tia's house and grab another change of clothes. Tia wouldn't be home, but the assailant might not be done. What if he tried to break in and trash her place?

As he drove his SUV back to the house, Jack found himself grinning. Tia thought he smelled good. She wasn't as indifferent to him as she pretended to be. He was making progress.

CHAPTER 19

"Get me out of here, Orion."

Tia sat on the edge of the bed, scowling at him. She was dressed in a loose pair of hospital scrubs, probably because it would have been too painful to pull her regular clothes on over her bruised body, and held her clothes in a rolled up ball in her lap. The pants stopped several inches shy of her trim ankles and the top ballooned around her slim torso.

Jack felt so happy to see her up and about, he grinned at her.

Her scowl deepened. "What are you laughing at?"

"Trust me, Tia, I'm not laughing. I'm just happy you aren't dead. Have you seen yourself in a mirror?"

"Yes. If you're done talking about my looks maybe you could get me out of here."

So. No sense of humor this morning. Jack could understand why. The woman had to hurt from head to toe. If possible, the swelling on her cheek and eye looked worse, the colors more intense with green and yellow added to the purple-red.

"How's Dozer?" she asked as the orderly pushed her in the wheelchair she had insisted she didn't need.

The entrance door swooshed open, letting in a crowd of

hospital visitors with various expressions on their faces—some drawn and worried, some frightened, one bursting with happiness and carrying a large bouquet of flowers.

"You can get up now, Miss." The orderly set the chair's brakes and Jack took Tia's hand to help her up.

"Stop scowling," he told her. "You'll give yourself premature wrinkles.

"Bite me."

The orderly smothered a laugh and wished them a good day before disappearing into the crowd.

"We'll pick up Dozer on our way to the house. I'm sure he'll be happy to see you." Jack had called Cass earlier to make sure Tia's pup had recovered. The vet sounded tired but had assured him that Dozer seemed fine, and was in fact running around her back yard with her boys.

Cass tried to hide her horror when she saw Tia's face and bruises, but her face was too expressive. She guided her friend to a kitchen chair and gently pushed her into it.

"Don't make me laugh, Cass—it hurts my cheek to smile," Tia told her. "I know how awful I look."

"No." Cass shook her head. "No, I don't think you do." She inspected her friend. "Nope. I don't think I've ever seen so many bruises on a single body. And your eye. Really, Tia, what were you thinking?"

"It wasn't my fault. I saw a pair of bolt cutters on the ground behind the pile of concrete forms and I thought they might have the fingerprints of the tire slasher on them."

Jack came to attention. "You found bolt cutters? You didn't say anything about them last night. Are you sure?"

"Of course I'm sure. I didn't mention them last night because I could barely talk if you remember."

Tia was not in a good mood. She hurt all over and her cheek throbbed. She had a doozy of a shiner and she didn't particularly like Orion witnessing her weakened state.

It didn't help that she felt like a fool. She had been so focused on the bolt cutters that she had let her assailant sneak up on her and take her by surprise. She had played the part perfectly of a stupid, weak woman who couldn't take care of herself.

She could have died. If Orion hadn't found her . . . . the reality of the danger she was in hit her hard. She shivered and gooseflesh rose on her arms. She wanted nothing more than to get Dozer and crawl into her bed at home and sleep until the pain and fear went away.

Cass must have known what she was thinking. "It's a good thing I called Jack or you and Dozer might still be laying there. Or worse. Your assailant might have finished the job and you'd both be dead. In my book Jack's a hero for searching the build site until he found you."

"I guess," Tia grumbled. She stared down at her scuffed leather boots. Protected by the boots, her feet were about the only body part that wasn't bruised or scraped.

"Ti-a." Cass gave her friend a hard stare. "Have you even thanked Jack for saving your life?"

"I can't remember. I was a little out of it last night." Not so out of it that she hadn't noticed how terrific the man looked in a tux. She had kept her eyes closed after that first glimpse so he wouldn't see the lust in them. "I need to go home and lie down. Where's Dozer?"

"Tia."

"Fine. Thank you for saving my life yesterday, Orion. I appreciate it." She was behaving like a churlish child and she knew it. She raised and dropped a hand.

"Oh, hell." She looked at Orion leaning against Cass's counter, his arms crossed against his magnificent chest, those long, strong legs crossed at the ankles. She owed him. "I really am glad you found me and Dozer. Thank you. I mean it."

"You're very welcome. We'll talk about what to do after you get some sleep. Let's get you home and into bed."

He saw Cass smirk behind Tia and almost smiled in response, but Tia chose that moment to stand. He wanted to leap forward and help her but he stayed where he was. If he treated her like a wounded animal she would snarl and snap at him. Better to let her know he understood how strong she was.

They collected Dozer from the boys after Griffin nearly brought Tia to her knees when he threw his arms around her legs for a "hug for her owies." Tia thanked him and Jack stepped in before the other two boys could innocently inflict any more pain.

Once home she visibly flagged when facing the two flights of steps to her bed.

"Allow me." Jack carefully picked her up and carried her up the stairs. He knew she had to be feeling like crap because she didn't fight him, merely curled into his chest and closed her eyes.

She opened them fast enough when she realized he had carried her right through her door, which she had left locked.

"I kicked it in," he explained before she could ask. "I was afraid someone had gotten to you. It was after midnight and you should have been in bed but you didn't wake up when I pounded on the door. So . . . I kicked it in." He shrugged one shoulder. "I'll fix it."

"Don't bother. I'll take care of it." She suppressed a groan when Jack set her on her bed. "You can go now."

"Not yet. I'll get you the Tylenol and a glass of water and feed Dozer, then I'll leave you alone to rest. It's Saturday so I'll hang around here today. If you need anything just holler."

Tia wished she could work up another scowl and send him away but she felt pitifully grateful that he'd be in the house. The attack on her the previous night had shaken her confidence. She needed to get over that, but at the moment she felt too bruised and tired to do anything about it.

"Thanks. Appreciate it. Leave my door open, please, so Dozer can be where he wants."

"Aye, aye, captain. I'll be right back with that Tylenol." Jack took Dozer downstairs with him and filled the dog's food and water dishes before heading back up to Tia.

She had discarded the scrubs and pulled on her favorite sweats and a faded ZeeZee Top tee shirt. Her eyes were closed so he set the bottle of painkiller and glass of water on her bedside table.

Her black curls framed her face, which looked pale and drawn beneath her light tan. He would have liked to draw up a chair and sit with her, but he knew she'd frown at the attention, so he went downstairs instead to make several phone calls.

Jack stopped by his office to deal with a few things first thing Monday morning before he headed to the Bayside build site. He hadn't left the house the remainder of the weekend except for a short run with Dozer on Sunday morning.

He grabbed his mail, handed Tamara's overnight bag to Ashley, and asked her to courier it over to Tamara's hotel. Tamara had tried to call him several times over the weekend but he had let her calls go to voicemail.

He knew she would be steamed at him. And rightly so, if he was honest. First because he'd abandoned her at the fund raiser, and second, because he hadn't answered any of her calls. Tamara didn't take well to being ignored.

He wasn't sure why he hadn't wanted to speak with her—maybe because he didn't want to tell her he was temporarily living at Tia's. She wouldn't like it, and he couldn't blame her. If the situation were reversed he'd be plenty pissed off, so he had taken the coward's way and asked Ashley to deal with Tamara's bag to avoid an ugly confrontation as long as possible.

Tamara didn't deserve such shabby treatment and would certainly tell him she never wanted to see him again. A month ago that would have bothered him a great deal.

Tamara Albrecht was everything an investment banker's wife should be: beautiful, gracious, intelligent, classy, and best of all, driven to make money. They would make a formidable team.

Marrying her would forge an alliance with Tamara's mega-wealthy father that would push Jack into the upper levels of the investment banker sphere. He'd be able to have a role in the biggest deals in the country–and in Europe. It was a heady goal.

Tamara had been dropping marriage hints the last few weeks, so he knew she was agreeable to the alliance. He had almost convinced himself that he should give up his bachelor lifestyle and ask her to marry him. Almost. He kept dragging his feet because if he was honest with himself, the prospect depressed him–he wasn't sure why.

Then he'd met Artemis "Tia" Smith and something in him had changed. After living at Tia's for the last two weeks he looked at Tamara with new eyes.

Watching her Friday night at the fund raiser he had realized how cool and reserved Tamara was. All of the time. Not just when they were in public, but in private as well. For Tamara, life was a series of carefully calculated duties.

Worse, Tamara didn't care about food–one of Jack's greatest pleasures–and didn't even appreciate his cooking, something he loved to do. Nor would she ever consider helping out in the kitchen. Using her hands for other than primping and greeting people was for lesser beings, not the Ice Princess.

Unlike Tia, who had shocked him with her calloused hand shake the first time they'd met in his office.

He couldn't picture Tamara running beside him, working up a sweat, or sitting at the kitchen counter dressed in comfortable old clothes and drinking a cold beer, or playing on the floor with a dog.

He shook the thoughts from his mind. He needed Tamara if he was going to accomplish his goal of becoming an important international player. It wasn't fair to compare her to Tia. Tamara was glamorous and cultured and incredibly beautiful. He needed to remember that. Keep his eye on the goal.

CHAPTER 20

TIA DRAGGED herself out of bed Monday morning after she'd heard Orion's SUV leave. She still hurt, but she was tired of lying around. Orion had insisted on serving her dinner in bed Saturday night, followed by breakfast Sunday morning. Much to her embarrassment, she'd let him.

Sunday night she had declared that she wanted to eat downstairs. Orion hadn't argued. He'd simply picked her up and carried her to the dining table, ignoring Tia's complaints that she could make it on her own, thank you very much.

He had, at her insistence, let her walk back upstairs after the meal while he cleaned up. Dragging herself up the stairs had been agonizing, and if she hadn't needed to prove something–not only to him, but to herself as well–she would have asked for help. She'd fallen into her bed with a sigh of relief and slept straight through the night.

Now she desperately needed a shower or she might have lingered in bed another day, despite being bored.

She adjusted the shower spray to a gentle pulse and let the steam and hot water work its magic on her aching muscles. When she renovated she had installed an in-demand water heater for each bathroom, something she especially appreciated that morning. She took advantage of the endless supply until her muscles finally loosened and she felt clean again.

She pulled on her second favorite sweats and a fresh tee, forgoing a bra because it put too much pressure on her bruises still, combed out her hair, and slowly made her way downstairs with Dozer at her heels. He had stayed by her side, sleeping next to her on her king size bed, except to eat or when Orion took him outside.

Dozer sat on his dog bed in the kitchen/dining area and looked forlorn while she made a cup of peppermint tea. At first she couldn't figure out why he wasn't happier to see her up and about, but then she realized he had lost his favorite rope toy.

"Poor baby," she said, reaching down to rub his ears. "We'll pick you up a new rope tomorrow. I promise." Dozer groaned and leaned against her, making her laugh. It was the first time she'd felt like laughing since the attack Friday night.

She took her steaming mug of tea and the Sunday paper she had yet to read onto the deck and turned one of the Adirondack chairs to face the sun, allowing herself the luxury of doing nothing but sip tea and soak up the warmth.

It felt strange being home and idle on a weekday. The neighborhood was quieter. Parents were off to their jobs and the kids were finishing up the last week of the school year. A dog barked on the next street over and Dozer raised his head, decided it was nothing and went back to sleep. Tia read the paper and napped.

Eventually her mind began to churn. There were things she needed to deal with. She needed to get her truck back. She needed to check on the bolt cutters. Were they still where she'd seen them or had her assailant taken them when he fled?

She needed to speak with the night watchman and Miles about making the site more secure—maybe even adding on a second watchman. She had tried to discuss these things with

Orion last night at dinner but he had shut her down, saying Monday would be soon enough to deal with it all.

Well, Monday had arrived and Tia needed to get back to work. She would have called Miles about her truck but she didn't have her cell phone. Jack had said something about tossing her canvas pack into his car but had apparently forgotten that he had it.

Tia read the remainder of the paper, then laid her head against the chair back and dozed again. The sound of a truck pulling up beyond her back fence woke her. She felt a brief moment of panic until she realized Dozer was standing by the back gate, wagging his tail.

Of course. It was her truck that she'd heard. Miles must have brought it back for her. She pushed herself out of the chair and started across the lawn to let him in, but the back gate opened before she was halfway there. Dozer barked and leaped in happy circles.

Not Miles. Orion's thick blonde hair glinted in the sun. She couldn't see his eyes behind the sunglasses he wore, but she saw the crinkles at their corners as he smiled. He was dressed for the office, in crisp tan khakis and a blue chambray shirt with the sleeves rolled to just below his elbow. The man had killer forearms.

"Well, good to see you up and about, lazy bones." Jack pulled off his glasses and inspected her face. "You look rested. Still have a nasty shiner though. Ugly."

Tia stuck her tongue at him.

"Oh, that's mature." He laid an easy arm around her shoulders and led her back to the porch. "Sit. Let's talk. Can I get you something to drink?"

"Stop treating me like an invalid. I can get my own drink."

"And she's back." He gave a gentle squeeze and released her

before plopping down in the chair next to the one she had just vacated.

Tia decided it was time to take control of her life again. "Thank you for returning my truck. Did you remember to bring my bag? I have calls to make."

"You call that ratty thing you carry a bag? That's not a bag, it's a rag sack." He held up a hand. "And yes, before you begin an argument you can't win, I have your bag. It's in the truck. I'll get it in a minute."

"I need my phone so I can call Miles. And the night watchman. And I need to check that the concrete form company is delivering the right ones today."

"Understood. You need to get back to work. Let's talk first."

She could either walk to her truck and get her phone or she could humor Orion and talk first. "I'm listening," she grumped.

"And so graciously too. First, I searched for the bolt cutters this morning. They weren't there. Are you positive you saw them behind the pile of forms?"

"Yes, I'm positive," Tia answered between tight lips. Why was he doubting her? "That's why I crawled in there, to pull them out."

"And you were jumped when you came out the other side of the pile."

"Yes." Tia went through the whole story again.

Orion listened, nodding now and then until she finished. He steepled his fingers and tapped his forefingers together, a habit of his that she had noticed he did whenever he was giving something serious thought.

"What?" she asked.

"A couple of things. I visited the guard this morning and inspected the flat tire. It had been intentionally punctured with a sharp object. I think whoever did it believed it would take him longer to change the flat. I also think the guard surprised your assailant when he turned up at the site sooner than expected, forcing him to hide your body behind the pile of forms."

"The guard had a flat and that's why he was late?" Much to Tia's frustration, Orion had refused to tell her anything about Friday night over the weekend. Now she knew why. The truth would have worried her.

She bit at her bottom lip, thinking. "I need to hire two guards, so they can cover each other. What if the assailant had hurt or killed the guard? I can't take a chance on that happening."

"I agree. Which agency did you hire the guard from?"

"None. Miles took care of it. I think the guard is a cousin of his or something. He goes to school days and needed a job that didn't prevent him from studying." She had the distinct feeling that he already knew all this. "What are you getting at, Orion?"

"Your assailant seems to know an awful lot about what's going on at your build site. It makes me suspicious."

"Of the guard? No. He's a nice kid." She looked at him and realized what he was thinking. "Of Miles? You think Miles is involved? Don't be stupid. Miles would never do anything to hurt me. We've worked together on several jobs and I pay well. Why would he betray me?"

Orion didn't seem to hear her. "Miles is dating my admin assistant, Ashley. Did you know that? They had a date Friday night. She asked me this morning if it was a conflict of interest. I told her no, but now I'm not so sure."

So Ashley was the hot new chickie that Miles had been so secretive about these last few weeks. Tia wondered where they'd met and why Miles hadn't wanted her to know he was dating Ashley.

"Miles is free to date whoever he wants. And he isn't involved in this."

"How did the assailant know you'd be alone at the build site Friday? I've lived here long enough to know your routine, Tia.

Miles usually waits for the guard at the end of the work day, not you. But Miles took off early for his date with Ashley. *How did the assailant know?*"

"I don't know the answer to that, but I know that Miles isn't involved."

Tia wanted to change the subject and she knew just how to do it. She reached down and pulled the society pages of the Sunday paper from beneath the chair. She had left it folded to show a photo of Orion and his girl friend standing with another couple at the museum fund raiser.

In the photo, Orion's tuxedo looked pristine, unlike when he'd shown up at her hospital room. His beautiful companion—the photo caption identified her as Tamara Albrecht—was a study in perfection. She wore a pale shimmering gown that skimmed a curvy body and stilettos that made Tia's feet hurt just looking at them. Diamonds hung from her ears and glittered around her neck and wrist.

Tamara had her arm linked possessively through Orion's elbow and smiled up at him. Interestingly enough, the woman of the other couple was also smiling up at Orion and stood closer to him than she did her own date.

The photo reaffirmed Tia's impression that Orion was a hound when it came to women.

Tia had seen Tamara's name linked with his in photo captions for the last six months. She knew the gossips were predicting a spring wedding early next year, but Orion had yet to mention Tamara's name to Tia.

She handed him the newspaper. "Sorry about interrupting your date. I'm sure your girlfriend didn't appreciate your leaving the party to rescue me. And I'm sorry about the tux. I'll replace it."

Orion didn't take the bait. He barely glanced at the paper.

Jack didn't want to talk about Tamara, especially with Tia. "I want you to report what happened Friday to the police. I took photos of you and Dozer in the bags before I pulled you out from between the fence and pile of forms. And I took a shot of you on the ambulance gurney for proof."

Tia felt a tiny stab of pain when Orion didn't deny that Tamara was his girlfriend. The pain grew into a solid dark mass when he told her about the pictures he had taken.

"You–you took photos of me? How could you?"

"We need proof so the police will take this assailant seriously, Tia. The pictures were necessary." He scowled at her. "I didn't take them to embarrass you if that's what you're thinking."

"No, of course not." Orion wouldn't do something like that. But he'd been clearheaded enough, even knowing she might be dead inside that bag, to take a photo. The knowledge depressed her.

CHAPTER 21

BY THE TIME Tia finished filing a report at police headquarters she was exhausted and aching, but she insisted that Orion go take care of his own business. She wanted to speak with Miles alone.

She found Miles sitting on the tailgate of his truck eating a large meatball sub. A neat eater, he wiped his mouth with a napkin and swallowed before he returned her greeting.

His eyes had widened at the sight of her face and his skin paled beneath his tan. "Holy crap. Orion said you'd been hurt, but I had no idea how bad. I would've come by the house to see you if I'd known."

Since Tia had never invited Miles to her house and had no intention of ever doing so she was glad he hadn't stopped by.

"Thanks, but I wouldn't have let you in if you had come. I spent the weekend in bed."

"With that louse Orion?" Miles wadded up the napkin and tossed it into a brown paper bag.

Tia frowned at her foreman. "My personal life is none of your business, Miles, but I'll tell you that I'm not sleeping with or dating Jack Orion. He's staying at my house until whoever is threatening me is apprehended."

That should have put her foreman in his place but he couldn't leave it alone. "Why Jack Orion? Why didn't you ask me to stay with you? I could protect you."

Tia sighed. Men could be so infantile. "For starters, you never offered, Miles. Even more important, Orion doesn't hit on me every time he sees me." Miles flushed at the direct hit.

"Beyond that, what I choose to do in my life is none of your business," she finished, her tone frigid.

Miles must have realized he had stepped over a boundary. He visibly swallowed and muttered an apology. Tia let him finish, then hit him with the reason she had stopped by the site on her way home.

"I hear you're dating Orion's admin, Ashley."

A guilty expression crossed Miles' face. "Who told you that?"

At least he wasn't denying it. "A little bird told me. How do you know Ashley?"

Miles fiddled with his sandwich but didn't take another bite. "She called looking for a permit. Rather than tell you I ran it over myself. I wanted to see Orion's office." He shrugged. "She's attractive and she flirted with me so I asked her out. We've seen each other a couple times."

"I see."

"It's my personal life," Miles added, defensive. "I don't tell you who to date."

Tia ignored the fact that he had done just that only a few minutes before. "Do you talk about what's going on here at the site with anyone?" she asked.

Miles shrugged one shoulder. "No more than usual. I bitch to my friends about problems like everyone else. Slashed tires, wrong forms. Harmless talk."

"What about Friday night? Who knew you were leaving early?"

It dawned on him then that Tia was after something. He pointed a finger at her. "You don't trust me," he accused.

"I need answers, Miles. I was attacked Friday night and hurt." She pointed to her bruised face and Miles winced.

"I know. I'm sorry about that, but you have to believe that I had nothing to do with it. I swear. Ashley asked me to pick her up a little earlier than we had planned because her brother called and needed to see her Friday night. She didn't want to cancel dinner with me, so we ate early and after I dropped her off I went alone to hear the band we had planned to see together."

He shrugged again. "Innocent."

Tia rubbed Dozer's ears while she thought about what Miles had told her. "Okay. I'm going to ask you not to discuss me with Ashley, just until we catch whoever is threatening me."

"Ashley has nothing to do with this. She works for Orion for crying out loud!"

"I know. Humor me, please. And let's hire another night guard to help your cousin. Use an agency this time, please. I want someone trained."

"Roland wasn't to blame." Mile's expression grew mulish. "He wasn't even here when you were attacked."

"I realize that, and that's why Roland still has a job. But the attacks on me are getting more serious, and I don't want him here alone. So hire someone today or I'll do it myself."

Behind her, the bulldozer engine revved. Lunch hour had ended.

Tia turned on her heel, patted her leg for Dozer to follow, and walked away from Miles before she lost her temper. It was becoming very clear to her that Miles might not be the foreman she needed. When she got home she would check the national database and see if there were any candidates available who could handle a multi-stage project like Bayside and were willing to commit to the five years the project would take.

After parting company with Tia at the police station Jack spent the remainder of the day in his office. He loved his office space—the way it sat out on a wharf, the view of the working and pleasure boats plying the waters, the smell of brine and creosote.

He watched a seagull spy something floating on the water, so close to his window that he could see its black eye. The gull folded its wings and dived, then bobbed like a cork on the water's surface as it gulped down its prize, its white and gray feathers glistening in the sun.

Jack took the contract he was reading to his couch and stretched out his legs. He loved negotiating contracts. He especially enjoyed ferreting out the hidden clauses the other side tried to hide in the long, excessive verbiage that gave them more than he was willing to give. Of course, he tried to do the same to the opposing party so he didn't blame them. It was part of the game.

His gaze drifted to the window again. He tossed the contract onto the coffee table with a sigh and took off his glasses, too distracted by his thoughts to concentrate.

He fully believed that Tia had been meant to die Friday night. Or at the very least, disappear. He needed to find whoever was after her before it was too late.

The last few years had been tight. There were fewer interesting building projects on offer. Consequently the Bayside project had drawn dozens of bids and designs from across the country. Those bids had been whittled down to three finalists.

Of the two losers, Jack dismissed one as too high and mighty to stoop to the type of thuggery threatening Tia. Just to be sure, he had checked into their upcoming list of projects and discovered that they were busy. Too busy to get upset over losing the Bayside bid.

The other company however, was a whole different story. It

was a local company, like Tia's Olympus Construction, and they needed work. According to Jack's sources (of which Tamara's father was one) the owner, Vinnie Garapolo, had several bank loans coming due soon and little chance of paying them off.

The Bayside project would buy him time and maybe save Garapolo Brothers. The question was, how far would Vinnie stoop to get the Bayside job? Would he kill for it?

The threats to Tia had started as more prank than threat– a cooler filled with rotting fish and a threatening note were not death threats.

The slashing of every tire on her heavy equipment was an escalation in violence. The note had also been more threatening.

On Friday Tia had been physically assaulted, her dog drugged, and both bagged. Jack's gut told him the assailant had planned to carry Tia off site in the bag. He may or may not have planned to take Dozer. It wasn't as if he'd be leaving a witness–the dog couldn't identify him.

Jack tossed his glasses onto the contract and stood. Since he couldn't concentrate on his work he might as well pay Garapolo a visit and see if he could dig up some answers.

An angry looking stranger stood next to Ashley's desk when Jack exited his office. Ashley seemed upset and she flushed when she saw Jack. He had the distinct impression that the two had been arguing.

He hesitated. He didn't have any appointments scheduled, but perhaps the man had shown up without one, hoping for an audience with him.

Jack veered toward Ashley's desk and stuck out his hand. "Jack Orion. Can I help you?"

The man set his thin lips in a grim line. "No."

He wore ragged jeans and old work boots. His snug tee revealed arms covered in tats. A green and black snake tat circled his neck and licked at his left cheek.

Jack narrowed his eyes. "In that case, perhaps you'd better leave my office." He wasn't about to let a strange man come into his office and bully his help. Especially this one, who had trouble written all over him.

Ashley's head jerked up. "It's okay, Jack. This is my brother, Trevor Hayes. He stopped by to see if I wanted to go to lunch with him but I told him I was too busy today."

Her eyes pleaded with Jack. He wasn't sure what she was asking of him, but he took her cue.

"Damn right you're busy. I need the negotiation contract I just edited retyped and delivered to Payne's office before two. You can take a late lunch after you drop it off." The contract wasn't ready, but he'd call Ashley after he got rid of the brother and tell her to forget it.

Jack gestured toward the door. "Can I escort you out, Mr. Hayes? I'm afraid Ashley isn't available for lunch today. I need her here."

Trevor Hayes scowled at Jack but realized he had no choice but to leave.

"I'll call you when I get home tonight, Trev, I promise. Why don't you have dinner with me?"

"Make sure you call. Don't even think about blowing me off." He walked out of the office without waiting for Jack.

"Trevor is your brother? There's not much resemblance."

"Different mothers. Trevor is six years younger than I am." She sighed. "Thanks for getting me out of lunch. I love my brother but he's been difficult lately."

"You're welcome. He seems wound a little tight." Jack hesitated. "Would he hurt you?"

"No." Ashley shook her head. "You don't have to worry. He needed to blow off steam about something. He'll be fine by tonight."

"If you say so. By the way, forget the Payne contract. It isn't finished. It was the first excuse that popped into my brain. And I think you'd better lock up after I leave. I don't know if I'll be back today or not."

"Is there anything I can do for you, Jack? You seem preoccupied lately. Is it–is it Miss Albrecht?"

"Tamara? Did you get her bag delivered to her hotel?"

"Yes. And she called while you were out. She didn't sound happy."

"No, I suppose she isn't."

Jack had no intention of discussing his personal life with Ashley. She was a fine admin, but lately he'd noticed that she had begun to hover, and looked at him like she wanted more from him. He simply wasn't interested.

Ashley was attractive and smart and efficient, but compared to the women Jack was used to dating she rated little more than average. Besides, he never fished in his own pond. It was bad business.

He heaved a silent sigh. He was going to have to let her go soon.

After he found a reliable male admin to replace her.

CHAPTER 22

THE VISIT with Garapolo yielded nothing. Jack had to tread lightly so as not to anger Vinnie Garapolo, so he mentioned Tia's troubles and watched for any reaction in the developer's hard, brown eyes. Vinnie insisted that he knew nothing about the lovely Miss Smith's troubles, but if there was anything he could do to help . . .

Jack wasn't convinced of Vinnie's innocence in the matter but what could he do? He had met with Vinnie in the developer's favorite restaurant, a small Italian joint called Rosario's that served excellent pasta but was reputed to launder money for the mob.

Given that the other "customers" in the restaurant were all big, beefy thugs who kept a close eye on Jack the entire time he was there, he tended to believe the rumored mob connection.

If Rosario's was connected that meant Vinnie was connected. Tangling with the mob did not bode well for Tia. Once the mob set their sights on something they rarely gave up.

Of course, at some point it wouldn't be worth sabotaging Tia's project. Even if Tia was personally driven off, her design plans would stand with her name credited.

Jack wondered if the concrete form company had been paid to intentionally send the wrong forms. It had delayed progress for close to a week and gave someone another opportunity to get at Tia.

Since he had no way to prove it Jack let it go.

He set off for Tia's house after the meeting with Vinnie. Now that he felt fairly certain that the mob was involved, it was more important than ever that she not be alone.

The problem was that he was only one guy. He had to sleep and he had his own business to run. If he didn't keep on top of all the projects he was investing in, or thinking of investing in, his business would suffer. They needed to get to the bottom of who was threatening Tia soon.

After making a couple of stops, it was late afternoon when he parked behind Tia's house. He was glad to see her truck there and let himself in the back door, disengaging the alarm. Good. She was thinking about security.

Dozer came galloping down the stairs to greet him, barking madly until he saw that it was Jack. Jack set his bags on the island, then knelt and rubbed Dozer's ears and scratched his back. "Tia upstairs, pal? Probably sleeping until you woke her, I bet."

"You'd win that bet." Tia stood on the stairs, her dark curls a wild mass around her head and her green eyes still heavy with sleep.

Even dressed in her old sweats and another of her faded tees—this one featured Jethro Tull—Jack wondered if the woman had any idea how sexy she looked. He doubted it. Tia seemed completely clueless about her sex appeal.

She took the last few steps down into the kitchen and put the tea kettle on. "I suppose it's too early for wine."

"I don't know why you'd say that," Jack said, pulling two bottles of chianti from one of the bags. "I feel like Italian tonight. I'm going to make you my famous puttanesca." He kissed his fingertips. "Bellissimo. Lots of garlic and capers. Why don't I open one of these bottles to breathe and pour you a glass?"

"Only if you have one too."

"Twist my arm." Jack reached into another bag and pulled a rope toy from it. He swore Dozer's eyes lit up as the dog's whole body went on alert. He removed the tags and handed him the toy. Dozer trotted over to his bed and immediately set to work on it.

"Thanks," Tia said, setting two wine glasses on the counter. "I meant to get one today and then spaced."

She watched Orion pour the wine, toasted him, and took a sip. "Mmmm, good. Just what I wanted. Do I have to wait long for your puttanesca? I forgot to eat today and I'm famished."

"I'll get right on it. Tell me what you did today."

Tia took a seat at the island to watch Orion cook. She hadn't wanted him to move into her house, afraid that he'd invade her privacy and be a nuisance, but it was working out pretty well.

It felt nice to have someone cook good food for her, and she'd discovered that she enjoyed having someone to bounce her day off during the evening meal. Orion understood the building business and he had brains. He made helpful suggestions and understood her drive to do her best.

The kitchen filled with the pungent scent of garlic warming in extra virgin olive oil.

Tia told him about her discussion with Miles. "He claims that Ashley needed to push their dinner date forward to accommodate her brother. I believed him. And he insisted that he doesn't discuss me with anyone. I'm not sure I believe him on that point, but I asked him not to talk about me with anyone, including Ashley, until we catch whoever attacked me."

Jack dumped a large handful of pasta in the pot of boiling water and stirred. "I met Ashley's brother today in my office. The man's a thug. He has a tattoo of a green snake circling his neck and licking his cheek. Not what I expected from a sibling of Ashley's."

Tia recalled Ashley's prim, buttoned-up dress and demeanor the day she had accused Orion of sending her the rotten fish and first threatening note. "No. It's hard to imagine your very proper admin with a thug for a brother."

She watched Orion pull down plates and set them near the cooking pots to warm. "You do know that Ashley has a crush on you, don't you?" she said.

Jack scowled. "Yes, and it's damned inconvenient. Ashley's a good admin. I'm going to be sorry to let her go."

Tia blinked. "Why let her go if she's so good? Ashley strikes me as an intelligent woman. Once you marry Tamara Albrecht, Ashley will realize that you're no longer available and her fantasy about you will fade." She shrugged. "Don't be too hasty. Really good admins are hard to come by."

Jack slammed the wooden spoon he was using to stir the pasta on the counter, making Tia start and Dozer get up from his bed.

"Who said I was marrying Tamara? What if I'm not ready to get married?" Where had that come from? Of course he was ready. Marrying Tamara was part of his grand plan. He had worked hard to woo her these past six months.

Tia held up both her hands. "Whoa. Sorry, didn't mean to hit a nerve. The gossip has you and your girlfriend tying the knot next spring. I assumed that was based on insider knowledge."

"No. There is no insider knowledge." Jack scowled at the cooking pasta. "Tamara is a lovely woman. And beautiful and intelligent."

"Soooo, if she's all those things, what's the problem? Or are you just not ready to settle down?"

Jack concentrated on dishing up their dinner and set the plates on the island along with a grater filled with a wedge of fresh parmigiano cheese. He poured more wine and settled onto the stool next to Tia and began to eat.

"Orion? If you aren't ready to get married no one can push you into it. But you should be honest with Tamara if that's the case. It could be embarrassing for her if everyone is expecting to see a diamond on her finger and none appears."

Jack shoveled a forkful of pasta he no longer wanted into his mouth. "I'm ready," he said after he'd swallowed the lump of food. "It will be a good alliance."

Tia secretly thought that any marriage that was based on the word "alliance" was doomed from the start, but she kept quiet and waited for Orion to continue. He changed the subject instead.

By the time Tia pushed her empty plate away she could barely keep her eyes open. The day's activities followed by two glasses of wine and a full belly had done her in. She told Orion that she'd clean the kitchen in the morning and headed for the stairs even though it wasn't even six o'clock.

She dragged herself up two stairs with the handrail and stopped to gather more energy. Orion chuckled behind her, then she felt his strong arms scoop her up.

"Looks like you could use a little help."

Tia curled into his chest and buried her nose into his neck. He smelled so good. Like spice and a faint musk that she associated only with him. "Thanks," she mumbled. "It might have taken me all night to get to my room."

Jack pulled Tia's comforter down with one hand, then laid her gently on the bed and covered her up. She had her arm wrapped around his neck and didn't seem to want to let go. Those big green eyes of hers stared up at him, so Jack did what came natural–he kissed her.

Tia's lips were warm and soft under his own. They tasted of tomato and garlic and red wine and something else that was uniquely Tia. He ran his tongue lightly over the seam of her lips to see if she'd open up and let him in. When she responded he pressed his advantage.

Not that he intended to let it go anywhere. Tia was still recovering from Friday night's ordeal and her bruises needed more time to heal before they engaged in the physical lovemaking he had in mind.

He pushed away the guilt that niggled at him. He wasn't married to Tamara yet. Having sex with Tia wouldn't be cheating, and he'd been up front with Tia about his intention to marry Tamara. He wasn't doing anything wrong.

After several minutes he reluctantly backed off the kiss and peeled her arm away from his neck.

"Good night, Tia. I'll see you in the morning." He turned away from the bed before she could see his erection and headed back downstairs to clean the kitchen.

Tia stared after Orion's retreating back. What had she done wrong? She pressed her fingers to her lips. They felt soft and slightly swollen. Orion's light beard had scratched her face but hadn't hurt. In fact, she'd liked the way it felt against her skin.

Her first kiss. No one would ever believe that Artemis Smith had never been kissed, but it was the sad truth. The boys she had known growing up were all her brother's friends and treated her like another one of the guys. It didn't help that her father was Zeus, the acclaimed Father of the Gods, and her closest brothers—Zee, Apollo, and Perseus—were also gods.

She might have had a shot at romance when she left home to attend school, but she had thrown herself into her studies and rarely socialized. If it wasn't for Cass, she wouldn't have a single friend from her school days.

After graduation she'd worked seven days a week to get Olympus Construction off the ground. The right time to date and learn about romance had never come for her.

And now she had Portland's most wanted bachelor living under her roof and she didn't have a clue what to do. No wonder he had stopped kissing her.

Tia wiped away a tear, pulled the comforter up to her chin, and told herself to look on the bright side. At least she had been kissed by an expert.

CHAPTER 23

AFTER TWO MORE DAYS OF delays the right concrete forms were delivered to the Bayside site. Tia paid her men overtime to get them set up and arranged for the concrete trucks to start rolling in the following day.

This was always an exciting, albeit stressful, time for her in the course of a project. The foundation created the base for what followed and therefore needed to be executed exactly to specifications. A few degrees off in orientation and the building wouldn't face the street properly.

The concrete used to support a building–any building, but especially a multi-story building–needed to be of high quality with no pyrrhotite in the aggregate that was mixed with the cement. Pyrrhotite was an iron sulfide that swelled when exposed to moisture and water, causing foundations to crack and crumble and eventually collapse.

Many a construction company had ruined their reputations by using substandard concrete. Tia swore she'd never be one of them. Her reputation as a builder who delivered a quality build under budget meant everything to her.

At her request, Miles had hired another night watchman to

work with his cousin Roland. The new guard came from an agency, had twenty years on Roland, and seemed competent enough. Miles still acted a little stiff and distant whenever Tia talked with him, but she figured he'd get over it eventually. At least she hoped so.

When asked, Miles admitted he was still dating Ashley. Tia didn't push him on it. His personal life was none of her business. Perhaps Ashley would fall for Miles and forget her crush on Orion.

No one had bothered the site since the night Tia had been attacked. In another two weeks, after the concrete cured, her framing crew would start work and whoever was behind the attack would more than likely give up.

Then Orion would leave and her life would return to what it had been before he moved in. An endless circle of work and solitary dinners. The thought depressed her.

Orion leaving should have made her happy. He took up a lot of space in her house.

Instead it reminded her of Orion's expert kiss and what it would feel like to take it further with him. She had waited too long to lose her virginity. The thought of having to tell him that she'd never been naked with a man mortified her.

Her steps faltered as a picture of Orion's hard naked body flashed into her mind.

Tia sighed as she headed to her truck with Dozer on her heels. She was such a loser. She needed to get a grip and stop thinking about sex with Jack Orion because he obviously wasn't thinking about having sex with her. If he had enjoyed their brief kiss surely he would have come back for more by now?

"Something smells good." Jack came through the back door, greeted Dozer, and wandered over to the stove to see what Tia had cooking. He'd been very careful not to get too close to her after the night he'd kissed her, afraid he wouldn't be able to resist pulling her into his arms and doing a much more thorough job of it.

"I was in the mood for comfort food," Tia replied, laying the top crust for her chicken pot pie over the filling and sealing the edges to keep the sauce from leaking out. "I made cranberry sauce to go with it."

"Yum. I'll open some wine, shall I?" Tia hesitated a bare fraction of a second, but he had become so attuned to her ways that he caught it. "Unless you'd rather skip wine tonight?"

"No, of course not. Please. Open a bottle and pour me a glass." It might give her the courage to execute her plan. On the way home from the grocery store Tia had decided to take matters into her own hands, even if it meant humiliating herself.

She didn't want to go to her grave a virgin, and Orion had the experience to get her past that embarrassing state. Given how women seemed to throw themselves at him she was sure he had bedded more than his share.

If Orion would be leaving in a few weeks then she needed to take advantage of him being under her roof. Unfortunately he seemed disinclined to seduce her, so she would have to do the seducing.

If she only had a clue how to go about it.

She gave him a bright smile when he handed her the wine glass and raised his own in a toast.

"So, how'd your day go?" Jack asked as he settled onto a stool to watch Tia cook. She shrugged and ducked her head. What was that about?

Tia wished she had thought to put on something more attractive than her old sweats and a faded tee. What had she been thinking? She hadn't thought her crazy idea through, that was her problem. She had been so focused on her mother's long ago advice that "the way to a man's heart is through his stomach" that she had automatically pulled on her comfy clothes before she began to cook.

Now it was too late. If she went upstairs and changed into a sexy outfit–did she even own anything sexy?–then Orion would know something was up.

Tia's plan to seduce Orion after dinner went out the window. She couldn't do it without help. She needed to retreat, regroup, and try again when she was better prepared. Attempting such a monumental task as seducing a player like Jack Orion required careful preparation. She needed Cass to tell her what to do.

As soon as she decided not to go through with her plan, she relaxed. She put the pot pie into the oven and did a quick clean-up. "Let's drink our wine on the front porch. I'll bring the oven timer with me."

They settled into the pair of grayed wooden chairs that Tia kept on the porch. She loved the Adirondack style of chair. They were roomy and extremely comfortable, and their wide, flat arms were perfect for holding a glass. She had purchased six when she bought the house–two for the porch and four for the back deck.

Although her street ran perpendicular to the Eastern Promenade and she lived only a block away from the park, it was a quiet neighborhood. Most of the houses on her street had been snapped up by Portland's growing yuppie population and renovated, or torn down and modern designs built on the old footprint.

Because very few had garages, the street was lined with Mercedes, Volvos, and fancy SUVs. Tia waved to her neighbor across the way as he exited his car, a young lawyer who had recently moved in with his lawyer wife.

"So, how was your day?" Jack asked again. Because he had

been watching, he had caught the moment back in the kitchen when Tia had relaxed. She had visibly let go of whatever had been bothering her. That didn't mean he intended to let it go. He didn't like knowing that Tia was keeping things from him.

They shared the events of their day while they drank their wine, talked about the addition of the agency-provided night guard to help Roland–an easy conversation between friends. Tia cocked her head and frowned at Orion.

"What? What'd I say?" he asked, scowling back. Why was she acting so damned strange tonight?

"Nothing. I was–I was just thinking that since you've been staying here we've become friends. It surprises me a little."

Jack's scowl deepened. "Why should that surprise you? I'm a decent enough guy. I like animals and I'm honest."

"That's just it. You *are* a decent guy. I didn't expect that from you. I thought you were . . . more shallow, I guess is the word I'm looking for."

"Shallow?" Maybe he was a bit shallow, but he didn't like having it pointed out to him, especially by Tia. "You think I'm shallow?"

"Thought, Orion. I *thought* you were shallow when I first knew you. But you aren't. You're a decent guy and my first real male friend who didn't come from my brothers."

Tia was sorry she'd said anything. Orion's face looked like thunder. He wasn't getting her point at all.

She tried again. "I'm glad we've become friends, that's all I was trying to say."

The kitchen timer went off and Tia shot out of her chair, grateful for the interruption. "I'll get dinner on the table."

Jack watched Tia head into the house, still scowling. Friends. Tia was glad they were friends. That should make him happy but for some reason it irritated the hell out of him. He wondered why being friends with Tia bothered him so much.

It only took a minute to come up with the answer. He couldn't seduce a friend. There were rules about that sort of thing. Friends were more important than a brief fling and were off limits. He'd just have to give up the idea of getting Tia out of her clothes and into a bed.

The knowledge made him feel depressed. He finished off his wine and headed into the house.

The sooner he got out of there and back to his own life the better.

CHAPTER 24

"Tɪᴀ, you'd look sexy in rags. Stop fretting. We'll find something, I promise." Cass patted her best friend's arm. She had never known Tia to be concerned about her clothes before–ever. Tia was the most unselfconscious female Cass had ever met. She put off shopping for clothes until hers were ready for the rag bin. And even then Tia simply tried on one or two functional pieces, bought them in several colors, and called it good.

Cass on the other hand, loved clothes. She had a closet full that she would have gladly lent to Tia if they'd been anywhere near a similar size. As it was, she and Tia looked like Mutt and Jeff when they stood side by side. Or Laurel and Hardy–one of those tall/short comedy teams. She picked up a pretty blue frilly blouse and inspected it.

Tia glanced at the blouse. "No. Too young looking. I want to look sophisticated. Orion is used to dating glamorous women. And exotic models. I need to measure up." A week had passed since her aborted attempt to seduce Orion while he was still at her house.

Shaking her head, Cass folded the blouse and set it down. The fact that Tia was so completely ignorant of how beautiful she was had puzzled Cass from the first day of their friendship. Had no one in her life ever bothered to tell her?

"Why do you call him Orion?" she asked aloud.

"What?"

"Why do you call Jack, Orion?"

Tia shrugged. "I don't know. I was angry with him the first time we met and I addressed him as Orion. It stuck, I guess. Why?"

"Just wondered. What about this, Tia?"

Cass held up a summery, soft teal sheath with vee shaped white lace inserts on each side of the waist. "Try this on." She tossed the dress at her friend. Tia gave it a doubtful look but took it into the dressing room.

"Nice. It looks wonderful on you, just like I knew it would," Cass said smugly when Tia emerged a few minutes later.

Tia looked at herself in the mirror and had to agree. The dress skimmed her hips and breasts and stopped several inches above the knee, showing off her long, tanned legs. The sleeveless design revealed well-toned arms and the lace inserts dressed it up.

"The color looks great with your hair and makes your green eyes pop. Buy it and we'll find a nice low-heeled but dressy sandal to complete the look. Jack won't be able to take his eyes off you. Where will you wear it?"

"Where?" Tia blinked. "I was just planning to put it on after work . . . " Her voice trailed off when she saw the expression on Cass's face. "No?"

Cass shook her head. "No. Absolutely not. You need to wear this out in public, someplace where other men will see you."

Tia frowned at her friend as she paid for the dress. "Why? I don't care about other men."

Cass took her friend's arm and pulled her from the store. "How can you know so little about men when you grew up with brothers? They're competitive. You want Jack to see other men ogle you. It will light his instinct to want you for himself. An instinct I personally believe is already lit, by the way."

"Nope, you're wrong there. He was kissing me and he stopped. If he wanted me would he have stopped? We were on my bed, for crying out loud, Cass. How much more convenient could it be for him?"

Cass spotted the shoes she was looking for and tugged Tia into the store to try a pair on. "I don't know. I wasn't there, but I'm telling you that that man is definitely interested. I could tell that the very first time I met him when you brought Dozer to me."

Tia scoffed. "You don't know what you're talking about."

Cass plucked one of the sandals from the window and gave a clerk Tia's shoe size, then turned back to her friend with a smug smile. "And how many boys did you date in high school and college? And which of us is happily married?"

When Tia didn't answer, Cass gave a curt nod. "I rest my case."

"Fine. You win. I won't wear the dress after work. What should I do then?"

"Take Jack out to dinner to thank him for everything he's done for you. No, wait–take him out for dinner for saving your life." Cass nodded, pleased. "Yes, that's it. Reminding him that he saved your life will pump up his ego."

"Orion doesn't need his ego pumped. He has a large enough one already."

"She'll take these," Cass said, after seeing the sandals on Tia's feet. "Sure I can't talk you into stilettos? Men love what they do to a woman's ass."

Tia laughed. "No, thank you. I'm tall enough already.:"

"That's one of Jack's plus points," Cass pointed out. "He's tall enough that you can wear real heels and not tower over him."

Tia ignored the heels comment. Cass had been trying to get

her to wear heels forever and Tia had never agreed to even try on a pair. "Plus points?" she asked, raising one eyebrow.

"Yeah. I developed a point system so I could rate my dates. You know, good hygiene is a plus, too much cologne or using chew is a minus. Like that."

"I assume Leonard collected the most plus points?"

"Oh yeah." Cass grinned. "He blew everyone else out of the water once we had sex. The man's a dynamo in the sack."

"Cassidy! Too much information." Gad, she'd never be able to look Leonard in the eye again without thinking about him and Cass in bed together. It was time to change the subject.

"What's a good restaurant? I don't want to take Orion to the places I usually frequent. It should be somewhere special."

"Take him to Marjory's. They do surf and turf better than anyone and it's always busy so you're sure to be seen."

"Okay, Marjory's it is. Are we done shopping now? I've had enough."

"Hardly. We're just getting to the good part."

"Good part? What more do I need? I have a dress and shoes." Tia hated shopping, unless it was for food or her house. The small specialty shops in Portland's Old Port district were better than shopping at the mall, but she could only take just so much.

Cass tucked her arm into Tia's. "I saved the best part for last. This is where you close the deal, girlfriend. Underwear plays a critical part in any seduction, and I'm willing to bet you're still wearing boring white old lady underpants and sports bras."

Tia flushed. Cass had hit the nail on the head.

"I don't see anything wrong with functional underwear," she grumbled.

"You wouldn't. Trust me, when you dress sexy from the skin out, you'll feel sexy."

"Fine. Let's get this done."

"Great." Cass grinned. "I think I'll pick out a sexy new teddy while we're there. Leonard loves it when I spring new underwear on him. He turns into a tiger in the bedroom." She laughed out loud at the look of horror and embarrassment on Tia's face.

"Come on, my prudish friend. It's time to further your education."

Tia wondered if she had ever been this nervous.

She didn't think so. Her stomach was balled up so tight she wanted to throw up.

She leaned on her sink and gave herself a careful look in the mirror. She had allowed her friend to talk her into a much needed hair trim and followed Cassidy's makeup instructions to the letter.

Would it be enough? A week had passed since her shopping trip with Cass and the night for her dinner out with Orion had arrived.

Her thick curls fell to her shoulders, creating a soft black halo around her face and head. She wore two shades of eyeshadow–sable brown and champagne–the lighter one in the crease and under her brow, the sable on her lids, and only a barely-tinted gloss on her lips. She had used a light concealer to try to hide the remains of her black eye, but the green and yellow discoloration still showed.

She felt like a painted lady, or worse, a clown.

The dress however, was a hit. She loved it. The peekaboo lace panels made her feel sexy, a new sensation for her. Ditto for her new thong and lace bra, although the thong was taking some getting used to.

She took a couple of deep breaths and wished herself luck, then exited the bathroom and put on her new sandals. This was it. She had no excuse to linger any longer. It was time to see if all her efforts were going to pay off.

She walked down the stairs with Dozer at her heels. Orion was standing at the counter checking messages on his phone. She watched him as she waited for him to notice her. He wore olive chinos and a blue polo shirt that brought out the blue of his eyes.

Jack glanced up and nearly swallowed his tongue. He pursed his lips in a silent whistle. "Wow."

He stared at her for so long that Tia began to feel irritated. "What are you staring at?" she demanded. "I can do dress-up when it's necessary."

"You certainly can. You look–" *ravishing. I want to rip that dress right off your body and take you right here on the kitchen floor–*"beautiful. You look . . . absolutely beautiful. Thank you for making an effort for me."

The ball of nerves in Tia's stomach loosened slightly. "Thank you. Cass helped me."

Jack grinned. "Remind me to thank Cass for her contribution to our dinner date."

Date? This was a date? The ball of nerves tightened.

"It's not a date, not really." She rushed to set Orion straight. Although she'd like it to be a date, so why couldn't she just keep her mouth shut? "I just wanted to thank you for everything you've done for me and Dozer the last few weeks. You know. Two friends having dinner." Shut up now, Tia. She clamped her lips shut.

Orion smiled, revealing the dimple in his left cheek. "Right. Not a date. Got it. Shall we go? I believe you said our reservation is for seven."

Tia nodded stiffly and started for the back door.

CHAPTER 25

"Not that way." Jack clasped Tia's arm as she walked past him and turned her in the opposite direction. She smelled terrific. "I brought the Mercedes so we can ride in style. It's parked out front."

Taking the Mercedes instead of her truck or Orion's SUV definitely put dinner in the date category. Tia felt a flush of excitement. "Great. Let's go. Dozer, you stay and guard the house." She set the alarm on their way out just in case her assailant decided to pay a visit while they were at dinner.

They rode to Marjory's in a comfortable silence. The restaurant was located in a beautiful old brownstone mansion on the opposite end of the city, near Portland's western promenade. Orion guided Tia up the wide granite steps with a light hand on her elbow.

Warm yellow lights glowed from the tall, ornate windows. Tia noted the multiple balconies supported by corinthian columns as she climbed the steps. The incredible carved woodwork inside the foyer took her breath away. A tall, stained glass window looked down on the foyer from its position on the first landing of a wide mahogany staircase.

"Wow. This place is incredible." Tia couldn't take it all in, there was so much to see everywhere she looked.

"I'm surprised you haven't been in here before. It's the kind of place every building designer should see at least once."

"It's not the sort of place you'd come to eat alone, and since I usually eat alone . . . " Tia shrugged. "I'm here now. I'll have to thank Cass for suggesting it."

Jack smiled. "It seems we both have reason to be grateful to your friend Cass."

The maitre'd approached. To his credit he refrained from staring at Tia's black eye, and led them upstairs to a dining room that held six tables. Four were already occupied.

The room had the same gleaming, hand-carved wood trim as the entry, an old oriental on the polished wood floor, and a crystal chandelier hanging from the ceiling's center rose medallion. Candles flickered on the tables. Tia found the room inviting and charming.

Menus were handed out, wine selected, and Tia settled in to read her menu. She was beginning to enjoy herself. Their wine came and she relaxed even more as they discussed their respective days and current news stories. She and Orion had never had a problem talking, she realized.

"My parents would love this place," Tia said with a happy groan as she bit into a perfectly cooked scallop. She looked at her dinner companion with a thoughtful expression. "I've never heard you mention your folks, Orion. Aren't you close? Or aren't they still alive?"

Jack shrugged one shoulder. "I have no idea."

"What?" Startled, Tia set down the fork that had been about to deliver another scallop. She patted her mouth with the napkin carefully, another little hint from Cass to help preserve her lip gloss.

"How can you not know? Are you . . . estranged?"

"You might say that. I have no idea who my parents are. I was raised by an old man who did what he could, but I'm afraid I gave him a hard time and he was out of his league. I left when I was sixteen and set off to see the world and make my fortune. I never looked back and now here I am. End of story."

He didn't look at Tia as he recited his little speech, eyeing the other diners over his wineglass instead.

Tia looked at him and frowned. "Only that isn't the end of the story, is it?" she said softly. "I bet you wonder who your parents are and why they left you. I know I would. Have you ever searched for them?"

"No. I think they made it clear how they felt about a child when they abandoned me to the old man. Let's change the subject, all right?"

"Sure. Tell me about Vinnie Garapolo."

"What do you know about Vinnie?" Jack asked.

"Not much. From my research I believe he's the most likely party trying to sabotage the Bayside project."

He forgot sometimes just how smart a woman Tia was. "I happen to agree with that assessment so I met with him a few days ago, but I wasn't able to shake anything out of him. He's definitely mob connected. He must have had a half dozen body-guards hanging around him."

Tia waited impatiently for Jack to cut and eat a piece of his filet mignon. "And?" she asked when he showed no sign of saying more. "Are you going to tell me why *you* think Vinnie Garapolo is our most likely culprit?"

Jack took a sip of wine. He often dined at Marjory's and enjoyed their food.

"Vinnie needs the Bayside project to save his construction company, which is on very shaky ground. Too many sub-par building materials that he's been forced to replace out of pocket.

He owes a lot of money, and if he doesn't pay up when the notes come due he'll lose his company. Vinnie is a desperate man."

"We can't prove it though, can we?"

"I'll think of something. Let's change the subject to more pleasant matters. That dress, for instance. What are you wearing underneath?"

As he'd intended, Tia forgot all about Vinnie. She blushed a deep red and his curiosity kicked up several notches. He was well aware that Tia preferred to wear the old-fashioned style of briefs and sports bras, but the fit and fabric of the dress she had worn tonight demanded better underpinnings. What had her friend Cass talked her into?

Jack's smile spread and a gleam appeared in his eye. "Come to think of it, I didn't notice any panty lines. You wouldn't be wearing a thong, would you, Tia?" He knew that he really shouldn't be pursuing this, but something in him drove him on. "You are, aren't you? What color is it?"

Tia mumbled something.

"What did you say? I couldn't hear that." Oh, he was enjoying this. Had he ever seen Artemis Smith embarrassed before? Surely not.

"Pale teal. Silk." Tia scowled at Orion. "So is my bra. They match." She was no good at this seduction thing. She might as well end the evening with as much dignity as she could muster.

The mental picture of Tia dressed in nothing but a few small triangles of pale teal silk popped into Jack's brain and shot straight to his groin. He barely stopped himself from groaning out loud.

Friend, he reminded himself sternly. Tia is a friend. He didn't mess with friends. He never should have asked about her under-wear. Now he wouldn't be able to get that image out of his head.

"Are we finished here?" he asked, his voice slightly strangled.

He took a deep breath and tried again. "I mean, I'm full, but if you'd like to order dessert they make a great flan here."

Suddenly Tia wanted nothing more than to leave. Seducing Orion had been a stupid idea. "I'm all set. Let's head home. I hate to leave Dozer alone for too long."

Tia paid the check and they headed down the curving staircase. At the bottom, just coming in, stood a figure Tia thought she recognized. They reached the bottom step and the woman turned around. Her eyes widened when she saw Orion.

"Jack! How lovely." Tamara Albrecht stepped forward and placed an arm around Jack's neck, then kissed him firmly on the lips. "It's so wonderful to run into you here, darling. I was just telling Daddy that you've been so busy I've hardly seen you these last few weeks."

If there was any censure in that statement, Tia certainly couldn't detect it.

Ignoring Tia completely, Tamara tucked her arm through Jack's and drew him toward an older gentleman who was handing off his hat to the maitre'd. "Do come say hello to Daddy."

Tia stood on the bottom step and watched the utterly gorgeous Tamara manipulate Orion. She was dressed in a silky, pale blue dress that hugged her curves and floated around nicely shaped legs. The woman was a walking wet dream.

Tamara had neatly cut Tia off from Orion, dismissing Tia as beneath her notice.

And why shouldn't Tamara dismiss her? Tia asked herself. She knew she was a fish out of water when it came to men and flirting. All she knew how to do was be herself. And that had never been enough to hold any man's interest. It certainly wouldn't catch the eye of a man like Jack Orion.

Jack gently pulled his arm free and patted Tamara's hand. "I'll call you in a few days, Tamara." He stepped back to Tia and took her elbow.

Looking into his eyes, Tia could read nothing there. His expression had shut down. She glanced at Tamara and caught her frowning at Orion. The frown smoothed out as soon as she realized that Tia was looking at her.

Jack led Tia toward the door, but before they could make their escape, Tamara's father recognized him.

"Jack! What a treat. Are you joining me and Tami for dinner? Naughty girl, she neglected to mention you would be here. We have a lot to discuss, what with the upcoming wedding and our business merger, eh? Good times ahead, Jack."

Tia wanted to melt into the floor, but she made herself stand tall and pasted a smile on her face. What a fool she'd been to think she could seduce Jack Orion!

Of course Orion was still going to marry Tamara. Hadn't he told her as much? When had Jack proposed? And why hadn't he bothered to tell her?

Now that Tia had met her, she could see why Orion wanted to marry the woman who stood before her. Tamara Albrecht was beautiful in her photos–but in real life she was positively stunning. Any man would want her for his wife.

They would make a lovely couple. The thought depressed Tia. She just wanted this farce of a date to end and get home so she could put on her old sweats and cuddle with the warm and loving Dozer.

"I'm sorry, Stephen, I can't join you tonight," Jack said, sounding truly sorry. "I need to escort my companion home."

Two pairs of cold, blue eyes fastened on Tia, obviously waiting for an introduction and an explanation. How would Orion explain her presence? She was tempted to introduce herself but kept her mouth closed. Let Orion handle it however he wished.

"This is Artemis Smith. She won the Bayside project contract with her neighborhood-friendly design. Bayside is one of my recently acquired investment projects," Jack answered smoothly.

He needed to get Tia out of there.

Stephen Albrecht clapped Jack on the shoulder. "A business dinner then." And with that he dismissed Tia as easily as his daughter had done. "I'm in town for a week, Jack. Let's get together tomorrow."

"I'll check my schedule and call you first thing in the morning, Stephen. Good night, Tamara."

Tamara stood on tip-toe and kissed Jack's jaw. "Call me," she said huskily. "I've missed you."

CHAPTER 26

THEY WERE ALMOST BACK at Tia's house before Jack spoke. "I apologize for Tamara and her father," he said.

"You have nothing to apologize for, Orion. They didn't do anything. I just wish you had told me that you had proposed to Tamara. It's the kind of thing friends share." She kept her tone light, even though she felt anything but.

It wouldn't do to let Orion know how much seeing Tamara kiss him had hurt. If she'd known they were engaged she would definitely not have set out to seduce him.

"I haven't proposed to her." His voice was gruff, angry.

Tia heard the unspoken "yet" at the end of his declaration. She turned her head to look at him. The light from the dash made the planes of his face look harsh. She could see a muscle working in his jaw.

"It's all right, Orion. Really. Tonight's dinner wasn't a real date anyway. Just a way for me to show my appreciation for all the help you've given me. Thank you for driving us to dinner."

She turned her head away so he wouldn't see the tears that had sprung to her eyes and stared out the window the rest of the way to her house. Once there she hurried inside ahead of him and flew up the stairs to her room. She desperately needed to be alone.

Jack followed Tia inside the house, well aware that she was anxious to get away from him. Damn that Tamara. He had enjoyed his evening with Tia. She was funny and intelligent and interesting. Warm. Incredibly sexy. Honest.

He liked that about her—that what you saw was what you got. Tia didn't play games. She was straight forward and told you what she was thinking. He found that refreshing and amazingly easy to be with.

She had attracted him from that very first day he'd met her in his office, but tonight had been the first time he had seen the truly feminine side of Tia and it had blown him away. That sexy dress skimming her body . . .

"Damn it." He didn't want to end the evening on a bad note. They were going to clear the air tonight.

He took the steps two at a time up to the third floor, rapped twice on the door and let himself in since neither of them had gotten around to repairing the broken lock.

All the blood drained from Jack's head when he saw Tia standing beside her bed dressed in only her bra and a matching thong, her dress hanging from one hand. He pointed at her before she could ream him out for entering her personal space without permission.

"Don't say a word."

He stalked over to her and wrapped her in his arms, pulling her body tight against him. "Not a word," he warned, his voice husky. He lowered his head and kissed her, teasing her lips open until he could taste her.

Tia's arms crept up and wrapped around his neck. He lifted his head and looked at her through heavy-lidded eyes. "I've been thinking about doing that all evening," he said.

Tia swallowed. Even with her lack of experience she could tell that Orion wanted her. "Me too. Could we try that again, please?"

Orion groaned something she couldn't make out, then scooped her up and laid her in the middle of her bed and stared down at her. "You are so beautiful," he said.

"No. Tamara is beautiful. I'm too–"

"I thought I told you not to talk."

He leaned over, placing a hand on either side of her body and kissed her again to quiet her. Then he gave her the more she'd asked for, until she was trembling and begging for a release from the exquisite tension building in her body. When she shattered he was right there to wrap her in his arms again.

Jack held Tia close. At that moment he knew that he couldn't take advantage of her even though he ached to have her.

"You haven't done this before, have you?" he asked softly. He felt her stiffen and try to pull away but he kept his arms locked around her.

"It's nothing to be embarrassed or ashamed about. But I can't be your first. It wouldn't be right. You deserve better."

Much to Tia's disappointment Jack let her go and left.

Oh god. Orion had seen her naked. More than that, he'd touched her most intimate places. Tia felt a sense of longing for more and at the same time she was relieved that things hadn't gone any further.

Did what happened count as having sex? It didn't matter really, did it? What happened had changed the dynamics between her and Orion. How was she supposed to act with him after letting him gain such intimate knowledge of her body?

She had to admit that she wanted more. She wanted Orion in her bed every night. She wanted to be the woman he chose to marry.

And that was the one thing she couldn't have. He was

marrying Tamara Albrecht. She needed to remember that Orion would never belong to her.

A sharp pain speared through Tia's body and made her shiver. She felt alone and stupid for letting herself fall in love with a player like Orion.

Because that's exactly what she'd done. She had fallen in love with a man who would never return her love.

Down on the second floor, Jack stepped into the shower. He felt frustrated and confused and angry with himself. He scrubbed at his hair until his scalp tingled. He enjoyed sex, always had. But giving Tia pleasure tonight without taking his own—that was something he'd never done before. And he'd never enjoyed himself more with a woman.

Jack toweled off and crawled into his bed but he couldn't sleep. Technically he hadn't had sex with Tia, but he still felt guilty. He planned to propose to Tamara. He had no business messing around with Tia. They were friends. Only friends, and he was determined to keep it that way.

What happened tonight was a fluke. It would never happen again.

He punched his pillow and shifted to his back.

He needed to get away from Tia Smith before she upset all of his carefully laid plans. In another week the framing would be underway on the Bayside project and the danger to her would have passed. Vinnie would give up and move on to other things.

Once that happened he could move back to his loft and get back to his life.

The thought depressed the hell out of him. He liked living with Tia and Dozer, but he had no future here. She didn't fit into his plans. He had grown up a poor bastard, getting into fights all the time because the other kids in his slum neighborhood teased him about the too small rags he was forced to wear, and the fact that he didn't know who either of his parents were.

He had fought hard for everything he now had–his business, his reputation, his bank account–and he wasn't finished yet. He was on his way to becoming a big, international player and nothing was going to stand in his way. An alliance with Stephen Albrecht was the ticket he needed to fulfill that dream, and that meant marrying Stephen's daughter Tamara.

It was a shame that Tia wasn't Stephen's daughter. Unfortunately, marrying a struggling young architect/builder would do nothing to further the plans he'd made.

Jack sighed. He never should have touched Tia. He neither wanted nor needed her to become attached to him.

One more week. Then they'd part ways and he'd never think about her again.

CHAPTER 27

TIA CRAWLED out of bed after a restless few hours of dozing and slipped out of the house for her run before Jack was up. She knew she couldn't face him until she had rebuilt her defenses. She didn't want him to ever know how she felt about him—she couldn't handle the pity she knew she would see in his eyes.

Dozer was his usual happy self, always up for a run no matter what the hour. The Eastern Promenade was nearly deserted except for the hard-core exercisers who pounded the pavement before their long work day began. Tia began to let go of some of her anxiety as her sneakers slapped the paved trail in a steady rhythm.

Birds sang in the shrubs and trees that lined the promenade's foot path. The boats moored off the narrow beach to her left rocked in gentle swells. Not a single cloud dotted the pearly gray dawn sky. The air smelled of saltwater and mown grass and gently cooled Tia's body as she and Dozer raced along the trail.

During the night she'd made the decision that she needed to ask Orion to leave her house. She couldn't face him every day knowing he was going to marry Tamara Albrecht. It was the right thing to do, she told herself for the dozenth time. She had to protect her heart. Once Orion was out of her life she could beging the process of forgetting him.

Then why, if it was the smart thing to do, did it make her feel so bad?

She reached the turn-around spot and headed back to the house, wishing she had somewhere else to go.

Her heart sank when she saw Orion waiting for her in the kitchen dressed in his running gear.

"You shouldn't be running alone," he said, his tone curt and pissed off. "I thought you understood that."

Tia barely glanced at him as she headed for the stairs and her shower. "I had Dozer with me. I was fine." She ran up the stairs before he could say more.

Standing in her bright glass and tile shower, she turned the water to scalding, scrubbing her skin until it turned rosy. Too bad she couldn't scrub away the memory of Orion's kisses and touch as easily.

She leaned her head against the hard tile wall. She didn't really want to wipe out the memory of what had been a magical night for her. She only wanted to not love the man. Falling in love with Orion had been stupid of her. Stupid. Stupid. Stupid.

Steam filled the bathroom and she welcomed the way it enveloped her and hid her from the world. She wished she could hide forever.

She turned off the water and stood dripping, unwilling to leave the warm safety of the shower. A large hand and a muscled forearm covered with familiar fine, red-gold hairs held out one of her oversize bath towels. Tia's heart leaped in her chest.

"What are you doing here?" she asked, grabbing the towel and giving him her best scowl. Orion leaned against the outside shower wall. He had dressed for work and held a mug of steaming coffee in his other hand. He held the coffee out to her.

"Peace offering. I'm not sorry about what happened last night, so I'm not going to apologize for that, but it can never happen again."

Tia wrapped herself in the towel and took the coffee. "I know that. I'm not stupid. You're going to marry Tamara Albrecht and I am—was—a temporary distraction. Don't worry, Orion, you haven't broken my heart."

Oh, what it took for her to tell that lie! She turned away from him so he couldn't read her face. "You can go now. I have to get ready for work."

"Right. I'll let you get to it." Jack hesitated at the bathroom door. "So . . . we're okay? Still friends?"

"We're fine. In fact, you should be able to move back to your loft in another week. We'll be far enough along that it won't make any sense for the city to change the design even if something happens to me."

She pasted a smile on her face and turned back to him. "Go. I need to get ready for work." She waved him off. "Thanks for the coffee."

———

Tia pushed her crew hard the remainder of the day, donning her leather work gloves and helping them to remove the concrete forms. She caught Miles giving her a speculative look several times, but he never approached her. Most of the crew gave her an extra hour, and they had all of the forms off and stacked for pick-up by the end of the day.

Tia had directed them to stack the forms near the front gate, not only to make it easy for the company when they picked them up, but also because she wanted to keep the fence perimeter clear for the night watchmen. The framing lumber and plywood had been stacked near the recently poured foundation for the same reason.

One more week, Tia reminded herself. One more week and Vinnie Garapolo would no longer be a threat. Of course, that also meant that she had to be hyper-vigilant this coming week.

She walked toward her truck after dismissing the crew, smiling and waving them off for the night. She felt exhausted. Not only physically–she had worked as hard as any of the men that day–but emotionally as well. She wanted this week over with and Orion out of her house so she could begin the process of repairing her breaking heart.

Maybe she'd go camping next week. Or visit her parents at their villa in Italy.

She tossed her gloves through the open driver's side window and knocked some of the dust off her jeans before climbing into her truck. The sound of a car horn at the gate interrupted her and she climbed back out.

"Were you expecting anyone?" Miles asked, joining her.

Tia looked up, surprised. "I thought you'd left. Where's your truck?"

I parked on the street after lunch." He didn't explain why and Tia let it drop. She really didn't care. They both stopped to watch the unfamiliar navy BMW stop outside the gate.

Tia hesitated. What if it was one of Garapolo's men, come to kidnap her? She waited beside her truck, ready to jump in it and run. Several minutes passed, then a familiar figure gracefully exited the vehicle.

Miles released a quiet wolf whistle. "Hubba! Who is that? Introduce me, please."

"*That* is Jack Orion's fiancée, Tamara Albrecht," Tia replied with sinking spirits. What on earth was Tamara doing at the Bayside site?

She reluctantly walked forward to meet the other woman. Miles started to follow but she told him to wait there. She had a feeling Tamara wanted to have a private talk. And she felt sure she knew the subject of that talk.

"Miss Albrecht." Tia greeted her cooly when she reached the gate. "What can I do for you?"

Tamara, her curvy body dressed impeccably in slim white linen slacks and a pale blue silk tank, looked at Tia's filthy clothes and disheveled hair and sniffed. "I needed a word with you, Miss Smith. Alone. I stopped by your house but no one was there, so I was forced to try here."

The way Tamara said "house" made Tia's home sound like a shack in a slum. Added to that, Tamara apparently felt it was Tia's fault that she had to track Tia down at her job.

This was not a woman Tia could ever grow to like, she realized. But then, Tamara was the most beautiful woman Tia had ever seen, and her father was richer than King Midas. Orion wasn't marrying Tamara for love, he was forming an alliance. Would he be happy?

Tia shook off the thought. It was none of her business. Orion was a big boy and he'd made his choice.

She inspected Tamara's clothing–pale blue must be the woman's signature color as she always wore it–and her perfect hair and jewelry and pale blue high heeled shoes with skinny ankle straps. Who wore high heels to a build site?

The tension began to drain from Tia's body. Tamara wasn't as perfect as she appeared to be. She might be the queen of a gala or the boardroom, but she obviously knew nothing about the joy of taking a barren piece of land and building something armed with only brains and physical labor.

Tia said nothing while she waited for Tamara to tell her why she had tracked her down. She heard the evening commuter traffic piling up on Forest Avenue. Horns blared and loud truck engines roared. Tia felt as if she stood in a small bubble containing only herself and Tamara Albrecht, separated from the rest of the world.

Tamara crossed her arms over her chest.

Watch it Tamara, you'll wrinkle that pretty silk tank.

"I just wanted to make sure you understand where things stand between Jack and myself, Miss Smith."

"That's really none of my business, Miss Albrecht, is it? If you'll excuse me–"

But Tamara wasn't done. "You shouldn't get your hopes up about anything developing between you and Jack just because he's staying with you to protect you from some imaginary assailant. He needs me. And we plan to get married in the spring."

Which is what the gossip columnists were saying. Tia suddenly wondered if Tamara had been their anonymous source. Tamara's words sunk in. Orion "needed" her? What about love? Didn't Tamara love Orion? Or want love from him in return? Interesting.

"Right. I get it. I really need to go–"

"Jack Orion is a man with very healthy needs, Miss Smith, and he isn't above taking advantage of a woman's . . . proximity, shall we say?"

Tia narrowed her eyes at Tamara. "What are you trying to say, Miss Albrecht? Please speak plainly. I don't do well with innuendoes."

Tamara pursed her lips. "Very well. If you and Jack have had sex you shouldn't read anything into it. Let me assure you, it means nothing. Since Jack will have no reason to contact you once he returns to his loft, I don't want you imagining there's more to your relationship than that. Don't make a fool of your-self by chasing after him. Besides, I'm expecting a marriage proposal from him within the week."

If possible, Tamara's icy blue eyes grew colder. "After we're married he'll move into Daddy's estate in Columbus. He won't be back. You'll never see him again."

"I see." Tia was surprised to learn that Orion hadn't proposed to Tamara yet. But then, he'd told her that, hadn't he?

She wondered what was holding him back. Obviously living at Tia's made it awkward. Most likely he wanted to wait until he returned to his loft and could have Tamara in his bed. The thought of Orion doing to Tamara the things he had done with her not twenty four hours before depressed her.

"If that's all, Miss Albrecht, it's been a long day and I have things to do yet. Thank you for stopping by." Tia turned away and headed back toward her truck, not waiting for a good-bye.

She thought about Tamara's little speech and wondered if Orion knew he was going to move in with Daddy after the wedding. Would he be happy in Columbus? What about his sail racing? And his loft?

She couldn't help but feel that the alliance with Tamara that Orion was so set on was going to prove to be a colossal mistake.

The knowledge did nothing to improve her mood.

"So, how did dinner with Jack at Marjory's go?"

Cass and Tia were sitting on Cass's back deck with a glass of chilled white wine. Leonard was giving the boys their baths and putting them to bed. Tia suspected her friend had sent him off in order to give them a chance to talk alone.

Tia set her wine down after barely tasting it. She had gone home after her unexpected talk with Tamara and had taken a quick shower. Unable to face him, she left a note for Orion before heading back out.

She had wandered around with no plan in mind other than to avoid the one person she most wanted to see. How pathetic was that? She drove out to Mackworth Island and put Dozer on his lead for a walk around the one hundred acre jewel, stopping to appreciate the small village of fairy houses that visitors built from whatever they could find.

Eventually she found herself parked in front of Cass's house. She hated to drop in without calling first, but she knew her friend would understand. Now they sat together and could finally talk but Tia didn't know where to start.

Cass looked at her with understanding. "Something happened, didn't it, Tia?"

Not trusting her voice, Tia could only nod.

Cass reached over and rubbed Tia's arm. "Was it that awful?"

Tears began to roll down Tia's cheeks. She shook her head. "It was wonderful," she whispered. "As far as it went."

Cass pulled back her hand and frowned. "It was wonderful? And you're crying? Those aren't happy tears. What gives?"

"He's marrying Tamara Albrecht. She came to the site after work today to make sure I understand that Orion is proposing to her within the week. They're forming an 'alliance'. And he's moving to Columbus, into her father's estate." She wiped away the tears and bit down on her quivering lower lip.

"Oh." Cass swallowed some wine and thought. "He hasn't proposed yet, you said. All is not lost. If you love him, that is. Do you love Jack Orion, Tia?"

Tia nodded miserably. "But it doesn't matter. Orion told me we can't ever . . . you know. He plans to marry her, Cass, and she's all wrong for him. She's like an ice queen, all cold business, and that's exactly what their marriage will be. Why did I have to kiss him? It was stupid. Stupid!"

She couldn't bring herself to share with her friend all that she'd allowed Orion to do to her body. That experience would become a precious memory that she would keep locked away in her heart. Something to bring out when she was feeling down and lonely.

"Our hearts lead us where they decide to go, not the other way around, Tia. You can't tell your heart who to love. I'm sorry you're hurting. I wish I had some wise words for you." Cass took her friend's hand again and squeezed. "It will all work out. Trust me. Love will find a way."

"Not this time. Business trumps love in Orion's world." Tia

stood. "I need to get home to bed. Orion is probably wearing a path in the kitchen floor with his pacing."

"So he cares about you."

"No. He cares about his investment in the Bayside project."

Cass shook her head at her friend. "For such a smart woman you can be pretty dumb sometimes. I've seen how Jack looks at you. He cares, Tia."

"I have to go." Tia called Dozer and left Cass's before her friend could sling any more platitudes toward her.

Orion had left the kitchen night light on for her and she saw a light in his second floor sitting room window. She disengaged and reengaged the alarm, refilled Dozer's feed and water dishes, and quietly made her way to the third floor.

Jack heard Tia come in the back door and move about the kitchen, then her soft steps on the back set of stairs. He willed her to stop by his room so he could see her, but she continued on up to her space.

He set down the book he had been pretending to read while he had waited for her to come home with a heavy sigh.

He had done the right thing that morning, telling Tia that there could never be more between them. He needed to marry Tamara. Stephen Albrecht expected him to marry his daughter. If he didn't marry Tamara now, after leading her to believe that was his intention, Stephen would ruin him.

What a mess. Jack considered himself an honorable man. He never dated more than one woman at a time and he always sent an expensive gift when he tired of them. He was scrupulously honest in his business dealings. He never cheated at games.

So why did he feel like a fraud now?

He laid the blame at the feet of Artemis Smith. He had been

living with Tia for longer than a month now. He saw her every day, ran with her in the mornings, ate with her at night, and never once had he felt even the slightest hint of boredom with her.

In fact, the more he learned about Tia the more he wanted to know. The longer he knew her, the more he liked and respected her. She was smart and hard working, warm and funny and real.

Jack sighed. It didn't matter. He was marrying Tamara. In fact, maybe he shouldn't wait until he moved back to his loft next week to propose. He had the engagement ring already, a pale blue diamond that he knew Tamara would love. It had taken his jeweler weeks to find the perfect color.

That's what he would do. He'd take Tamara to dinner tomorrow night and pop the question. He already knew she'd say yes–she'd told him as much.

Jack punched in Tamara's number and made the dinner date. Seven at Marjory's, a private dining room. Champagne. Candlelight.

He ended the call and looked in the bathroom mirror. The face that looked back at him was not that of a happy man. He scowled at himself.

Buck up, you idiot, he told the man in the mirror. You're about to become engaged to one of the most beautiful women on the planet. The alliance with her father will catapult you into the top tier of development investing.

Jack crawled into his bed and stared at the ceiling. Tia's bed sat almost directly over his. He pictured her long lean body, naked beneath his, and the warm, eager passion she had shyly shown the previous night.

He swore and punched his pillow, then forced his mind to focus on his upcoming engagement dinner.

"I have a date with Ashley tonight," Miles told Tia at the end of the following work day. The second day during which Tia had done her best to work herself to the point of exhaustion in the hopes that she could finally sleep without thinking or dreaming about Orion.

She smiled at Miles. "And I suppose that means you want to skip out early?" She waved a hand at him. "Go. I'll wait for Roland and Mark."

"You sure? I can stay. I'm sure Ashley will understand."

But Miles didn't look like he wanted to stay. Tia knew that he and Ashley were seeing each other nearly every night now. Maybe Miles had finally found a woman he was willing to settle down with.

She did wonder, if they were seeing each other so often, why Miles needed to leave early.

As if he'd read her mind, he hastened to explain. "We're doing the special Island Ferry dinner cruise tonight," he explained. "They leave the dock at six-thirty sharp."

"Ah, I see. That's pretty romantic I hear. Sounds as if you and Ashley are getting pretty serious," she teased.

Miles blushed. "Yeah, well. I really like her. A lot. She doesn't bore me, you know?" He shrugged. "I'm not sure if we'll end up at the alter, but I'm willing to stick long enough to find out."

"That's great, Miles. I'm happy for you. Go. I'll be fine until Roland and Mark show."

Miles hesitated. "I shouldn't leave you alone."

"I'm not alone. I have Dozer. We'll wait for the guards by my truck. Go. Have a great time."

As she knew he would, Miles grinned at her and took off. Tia sat on the tailgate of her truck and inspected the build while she waited. They had started framing today. In another week it would begin to resemble a building. Or the first floor would at least.

She pictured the way the place would look when finished, with brick sidewalks winding through the complex and old-fashioned street lamps, lots of shrubs and flowers and shade trees with quaint shops and small businesses. It made a lovely image.

The sound of two engines driving through the gate interrupted her thoughts. She looked over and saw Mark pulling in in his big red Dodge Ram. A macho truck for a man who wanted to be seen as a macho guy. She hadn't warmed up to Mark, but she didn't need to befriend all of her workers, although she tended to.

Tia expected to see Roland's Rav following the truck, but saw a Hyundai sedan driven by a stranger instead. She slid off the tail gate but stayed by her truck and waited for Mark to come to her.

He parked on one side of her truck and the Hyundai slid in on the other.

"Evening, Tia," Mark said, joining her. "Where's Miles?"

"He had a hot date and left early." Tia nodded at the guy still sitting in the Hyundai. "Where's Roland?"

"Sick. I called up a buddy of mine to fill in tonight if it's all right with you."

"Yes. I don't want you here alone. Introduce me please."

"Sure thing." Mark walked to the Hyundai and rapped on the window. He jerked his head toward Tia. "Come meet the boss."

Tia inspected the stranger as he approached her. His jeans were worn and his arms covered with tats. A green and black snake circled his neck, its head and tongue flicking out across the man's cheek as if tasting him. Creepy.

She'd take him for tonight as it was too late to get someone else, but if Roland wasn't better by tomorrow she'd call the agency and hire a sub. She held out a hand. "I'm Tia Smith."

"Trevor Hayes." Trevor dropped her hand and stepped back.

"Well, I guess I'd better get going." She felt uneasy and had a strong urge to get out of there. Was she so shallow that the sight of Trevor's tats put her on edge? Tia opened the passenger door for Dozer and belted him in. She closed the door and turned, only to find Trevor standing in her way.

"Excuse me," she said, and started to push by.

Trevor grabbed her arm with one hand and shoved a wet, sweet-smelling rag over her nose and mouth. Tia tried to push it away but she didn't have the strength. She grew dizzy. Her legs buckled and she fell to her knees. Dozer was barking in the truck.

"Pop your trunk," she heard Mark say. Then . . . nothing.

CHAPTER 29

JACK PULLED his roadster in front of Tamara's hotel and tipped the valet to keep it waiting for him. "I'll be right back," he told the eager college student. The valet looked momentarily disappointed that he wouldn't get a chance to drive Jack's car, but he cheered up considerably when he saw the size of the tip Jack squeezed into his hand.

Jack strode into the hotel lobby, a richly appointed space with thick carpets, leather seating areas, and large vases filled with fresh flowers. A bank of mirrored elevators lined the back wall. To his right a piano player played softly in the lodge.

Jack stopped at the desk and asked the clerk to inform Miss Albrecht that he was here to pick her up.

He didn't sit in any of the comfortable chairs, choosing instead to stand in the entryway of the lounge where he could watch the young woman behind the piano. His hand fiddled in his pocket with the ring. The ring. Tonight he was going to become affianced to the beautiful Tamara.

He should feel ecstatic. His carefully laid and executed plans were all bearing fruit. Why then did he feel he was missing something important?

The elevator dinged behind him and he turned to watch the woman he planned to marry walk toward him. She wore a simple ice blue sheath and sky high matching heels. Diamonds dripped from her ears and circled her wrist and neck. She looked exquisitely beautiful and he was the luckiest guy on the planet.

Why then was he suddenly picturing Tia after a day at the build site–her dirt-smudged face grinning at him, her moss green eyes sparkling with excitement. Her whole being alive and engaged.

He frowned slightly at that last thought. Did Tamara ever become fully engaged with anything that wasn't business?

"Darling, what's wrong?"

Jack smoothed out his face and took Tamara's arm. "Nothing. I thought I had forgotten to answer an important memo, but I recalled that I handled it yesterday."

Tamara patted his arm. "Of course you took care of it. You are an excellent businessman, Jack. You and Daddy are going to rule the world together."

"I'm not sure I want to rule the world, Tam," Jack replied, ignoring her grimace at the shortening of her name as he handed her into his car, "but I do look forward to doing business with your father."

They rode in silence until they were almost to Marjory's. "I saw your roommate yesterday," Tamara said.

Jack's head jerked to the right. "What? Where?"

"I stopped by her build site and spoke to her. Artemis Smith, right? Such an ugly name for a woman. Not that she looked very womanly dressed in boots and jeans and covered with dust and dirt." Tamara gave a delicate little shudder. "I imagine you'll be glad to finally rid yourself of her."

Jack ignored the urge to defend Tia's name and dress. Tia worked hard for her living, something a spoiled princess like

Tamara could never understand. He knew there was no point in wasting his breath.

"Why did you go see Tia?" he asked.

"I felt she needed to understand the situation."

"What situation?"

"She needed to know that we have an understanding." Tamara smoothed an imaginary wrinkly from her dress. "I also told her that you'd be moving to Columbus after we marry, so she should let go of any illusions she might hold about maintaining any sort of relationship with you after you move out of that ugly house of hers."

Jack clenched his jaw to hold in any angry words he might regret later. No wonder Tia hadn't wanted to talk to him the previous night. He stifled a sigh. He needed to stay focused on the prize. Marriage to Tamara, business with Daddy. The sooner he moved out of Tia's the better.

"Jack?"

"Yes?"

Tamara turned her elegant head and looked at Jack. "I'm not opposed to you keeping a mistress or two after we're married, as long as it's done quietly and she isn't someone embarrassing like Artemis Smith."

"What!?" The steering wheel jerked in Jack's hands and he cursed. He spied an empty space curbside and pulled in, setting the car to park. Only then did he turn to look at Tamara.

She looked back at him, all cool, calm beauty. "I'm not really interested in that aspect of our relationship, you see," she explained.

Jack sat, dumbfounded. It was true that Tamara had been cool and distant the few times he'd bedded her, but he had assumed that would change as they grew to know one another better.

The idea of taking a mistress after marriage had never crossed his mind. He was a one woman at a time man. Always had been, and he fully intended to remain faithful to his wedding vows.

A sudden image of Tia's athletic body riding him, her head thrown back with passion, her black curls bouncing around her shoulders, flitted through his brain. He felt as if all the air had been sucked from the car. His head buzzed as if it had been invaded by a swarm of angry bees.

"Jack?" Tamara placed a hand on his thigh. "I thought I should let you know that I don't mind. I know a man like you has a healthy appetite for . . . that sort of thing." She patted his thigh a couple times and withdrew her hand. "I'm just not interested. Don't you think we should get moving if we're going to make our dinner reservation? I'm looking forward to seeing the ring you chose."

Jack made no move to drive on. "You don't care if I keep a mistress after we're married."

"No. It's a sensible arrangement. I'll keep my bedroom at Daddy's, of course. There are plenty of others for you to choose from for yourself. Naturally you'll have to keep an apartment for your mistress. It wouldn't be right to bring her into Daddy's house."

"Let me ask you something, Tamara. Do you love me?"

Tamara gave a little laugh. "Jack, why would you ask such a thing? Our marriage is a business arrangement. I like you well enough to marry you and that's sufficient."

A picture of his future life–a cold businesslike marriage, no children to love and play with–Jack shuddered. He had grown up without parents to love him. He *wanted* a family. He wanted a woman to love and make love with. A woman who loved him, not the bottom line on his account sheets.

He faced forward and put the car in gear, looked both ways and executed a u-turn.

"Where are we going? Did you forget something?" Tamara asked.

"Yes. I forgot something. I nearly forgot what's really important in life." He pulled up in front of Tamara's hotel, got out, and opened the passenger door. Before Tamara could say anything more, he undid her seatbelt and gently pulled her from the car by her elbow.

"This won't work between us," he said. "I'm sorry, although I should thank you. You've helped me realize that I need more—that I need love in my life. I need to give it, and I need to receive it."

Tamara stiffened. Her already pale cheeks paled further, and if possible, her icy eyes grew icier. "So, this is good-bye, then. I'm sorry I wasted so much time on you, Jack. Daddy won't be pleased."

"No, I imagine he won't. Fortunately I haven't entered into any business dealings with him yet so we'll all be able to avoid one another. Goodbye, Tamara. I'm sure you'll find another businessman who will be more than happy to marry you and Daddy."

Jack turned and sprinted around the front of the car. He needed to go home. He needed to see Tia and ask her if she might be able to learn to love him. She was unlike any other woman he'd ever met. Intelligent, interesting, dedicated, passionate, loyal, loving. And beautiful. So beautiful, inside and out.

They had become friends, and if she would have him, they could also be lovers.

One thing was blazingly clear to him now.

In the last month he had not only grown to love Tia Smith, he had fallen head over heels *in* love with her.

He wanted to marry her. To make a family with her.

To spend the rest of his life with her.

He gunned the car and headed home.

CHAPTER 30

TIA OPENED her eyes and immediately closed them again as a wave of nausea washed over her. She lay on a hard surface with her hands tied behind her.

She took several deep breaths to clear the sick feeling and smelled cat litter, stale beer, and fried food. Swallowing against the bile that rose into her throat, she opened her eyes again.

She was in a small room, more of a large closet really, with thin, stained wall-to-wall carpet that felt rough beneath her cheek. Pulling her knees to her chest, she rolled onto them and lifted herself up to a kneeling position. Her head throbbed in protest.

What was she doing there? Memory returned while she waited for the throbbing to subside. She'd been speaking with Mark, the night guard, at the build site. He had hired a replacement for Roland because Roland was sick.

An image of a heavily tattooed man with a green and black snake licking his cheek flashed into her mind. She shuddered.

The temp guard had held a smelly rag to her face. After that–nothing.

He must have used chloroform on her and kidnapped her.

Mark hadn't stopped the man. That meant Mark was part of the kidnapping.

What had they done with Dozer? Had they hurt him?

Tia strained her wrists against the plastic zip tie but it held tight. She plopped down on her heels and looked around her prison. She needed to escape. She had to find Dozer. If Mark had hurt her dog–well, there was no telling what she'd do in retribution.

A dim crack of light filtered in at the bottom of a door and at the top edge of a window. The room contained no furniture other than a dumped kitty litter tray. Judging from the odor, and the mounds of litter-crusted poop on the floor around the tray, Tia doubted it had been cleaned within the the previous year–or longer.

The room's walls and ceiling were badly stained, the faded red flocked wallpaper hanging off in wide strips. A single, unlit bulb hung from the center of the ceiling on frayed wires. Fire hazard. Chunks of the ceiling had fallen to the floor, exposing thin wooden slats.

The room had all the earmarks of being in a condemned building.

There had to be a dozen or more condemned buildings in Portland. But since she had no idea how long she'd been unconscious, Tia knew that she could very well be outside of Portland as well.

A sheet of half inch plywood covered the room's only window. She turned her head and eyed the door. Solid wood. Too bad. If it had been one of the cheap hollow core doors she might have been able to kick through it. She'd still try, of course, once she learned all she could of her prison.

She'd been kidnapped. She still couldn't believe how easily it had been done.

She lifted herself up again and stood, waiting for another

wave of nausea to pass. She wished she had some water to settle her stomach. Her tongue felt dry and seemed to fill her mouth.

Ignoring her thirst, she tiptoed over to the door and pressed her ear against it. At first she heard nothing, but then she heard the unmistakable sound of canned laughter. Someone was outside the room watching television, or perhaps a video on their phone or a laptop. If the building was condemned there'd be no power available, so it had to be a portable device.

Tia stepped away from the door and tiptoed over to the window, testing each step to make sure the floor would hold her. A condemned building was deemed unsafe by the building inspectors. By the looks of it, she guessed this one had been condemned for a while. She had no desire to fall through the floor, especially without the use of her hands to break her fall.

The sheet of plywood reaffirmed her theory that she was being held in a condemned building. Why else cover the window? A close inspection told her the plywood had been screwed firmly to the window frame.

She turned her back to the plywood and worked her fingers under one corner. There was a half inch or so of space because of the window trim, but no matter how she pulled the plywood didn't move.

Tia gave up and pressed her ear to the plywood. She heard nothing for a frustrating length of time, then the airbrakes of an eighteen wheeler blasted not far from her.

The truck's noisy brakes had given her two pieces of information. She was on the first floor of the building, and it was located in a commercial/mixed use area. The room she was trapped in belonged to a house, not a commercial business. Businesses didn't decorate with red flocked wallpaper.

That meant she could be in several areas on the outskirts of Portland.

Tia tried to think of what to do next. The door was guarded

and the window firmly blocked. She couldn't use either of them to escape. What did that leave?

She looked up at the falling ceiling. Thin, gray wooden slats showed where the plaster had crumbled away. This was an older building then, built before sheetrock came into fashion. But even if she thought the ceiling would hold her she had no way to climb without the use of her hands.

Could she push through one of the walls?

Starting at the right hand edge of the plywood, Tia worked her way along one wall, pressing against the wall with her shoulder, hip, and knees as she felt for soft spots. She would have liked to kick at the baseboard as well, but was afraid the noise would draw attention.

When she reached the door she stopped to listen again but heard nothing. Had the kidnapper left?

Dropping to her knees, Tia pressed her eye against the keyhole. At first she could make out very little in the dim space beyond, but then she recognized the outline of a bare mattress against the far wall. Empty cans and fast food bags littered the floor.

Was her kidnapper squatting in the condemned building? Unfortunately the keyhole limited how much she could see of the next room. She stood and pressed her ear against the door again to listen. After several minutes of silence she decided he had left.

She stepped quickly to the opposite wall and ran at the door, slamming her shoulder against it. She bounced back with a painful cry, her shoulder throbbing. She wasn't big and strong enough to break down a door with her shoulder. And now that she inspected it more closely, she saw that the door opened into the room. Battering it would do nothing but beat up her body.

Tia gave the door a few vicious kicks anyway, in case the lock was flimsy and she could somehow spring it open, but nothing happened. Older buildings were built much more solidly than their modern counterparts and this one had been no exception.

She leaned against the door, careful to avoid her bruised shoulder, and let her gaze roam around the room.

Hopeless. Escape was hopeless.

What did they plan to do with her? They could leave her here to die and nobody would know.

Or they could kill her.

A cold chill ran down Tia's spine. She could identify her kidnapper and Mark. If they left her alive–no, they wouldn't.

Jack would know something had happened to her. Tia felt confident that Jack would turn Portland upside down when she didn't come home tonight. The thought gave her little comfort. What were the chances he'd think to search this particular condemned building?

What if Jack didn't go home tonight? He had a hot date with the lovely Tamara Albrecht, his almost-fiancé. He might spend the night with her at her hotel. Or take her home to his loft apartment.

Thoroughly depressed by the thought of Jack and Tamara in bed together, Tia clunked her face onto the edge of the door.

"Ow." She had caught her cheek on a piece of cold metal.

She jerked her face back and stared at the door hinge that had hurt her. Of course, if the door opened into the room then the hinges had to be on this side of the door frame. Could she pull one loose?

Tia spun around and backed up to the frame, feeling with her hands. She felt the smooth round top of the pin that held the two parts of the hinge together and tried to work her short nails under its edge. After several frustrating attempts she had enough of a grip to try pulling.

She went to work.

CHAPTER 31

JACK SAT in his car and stared at the empty spot where Tia's truck should have been parked. Where the devil was she? He checked his watch. It was after eight o'clock. She should be home by now.

He strode through the back yard and let himself into the house, deactivating the alarm. A quick look told him Tia's work boots and the ratty bag she carried were missing as well. Had she been home at all?

He took the back stairs two at a time. Pulling off his suit jacket and tie as he climbed, he tossed them in the direction of his rooms and continued up to the third floor.

The lock on Tia's door still hadn't been repaired. He yanked open her door and entered her space. It still smelled faintly of her morning shower–the herbaceous scent of her favorite sandal-wood soap seemed to float about the large, open space.

Her camping gear lay in the corner where he'd noticed it the night he and Tia had made love–Jack shut down his thoughts. She wasn't here and neither was Dozer. They weren't out for a run–her running shoes were on the boot tray next to the back door.

He whipped out his phone and found Cassidy's number.

"Cassidy. Jack. Is Tia with you?" He paced to the windows overlooking Portland's Back Bay area and tried to locate the build site.

"Tia should be home by now, Jack. Why?"

Cassidy's voice sounded a little cool and Jack knew that Tia had told her they had slept together.

"She's not here and I'm worried about her," he said. "It doesn't look like she came home after work. Her work boots are missing. Did you talk to her today? Was she all right?" He heard his voice catch and cursed silently.

"Jack." Cassidy said nothing more for a moment. "What are your intentions toward Tia? She's my closest friend and I don't want to see her hurt, although I suspect it's already too late."

"I love her and I want to marry her. But I can't tell her that until I find her. Is she with you?" *Please be at Cass's*, he prayed.

"I'm sorry, but she isn't here, Jack. I talked to her–" Jack heard one of the boys yell in the background. "Hold on a minute, please. Carter's upset about something."

Jack waited impatiently for Cassidy to deal with her son's problem. She sounded upset when she came back to the phone after several long minutes.

"You still there?" she asked.

"I'm here. Look, Cassidy, I have to go. I need to find Tia."

Cassidy talked right over him. "Carter just came in with Dozer. He's limping and has a bloody nose and neither Tia nor her truck is parked on our street."

Jack was already running down the stairs. "I'll be there in five minutes." He shut off his phone, reset the alarm, and jumped in his SUV. Four minutes later he was pounding on Cassidy's front door.

"Where is he?" he demanded, brushing past Carter when he opened the door.

"Mom has him in her office." Carter led the way through the house and into Cassidy's clinic with Jack close on his heels.

"Dozer, boy." Jack rubbed the dog's ears with his large hands. Dozer whined in response. "Nothing serious?" he asked Cassidy.

Cass put away the bottle of antiseptic she had used to treat Dozer's wounds. "A small cut on his right front paw and an abraded nose." She looked at Jack, her eyes filled with worry. "Something's happened to Tia. She would never let Dozer wander the streets alone."

"I agree. Tell me when you talked with her last and what she said." Still on the examining table, Dozer leaned against Jack and whined again. Jack wrapped his arms around the dog's large chest. "We'll find her, Doze, don't worry," he murmured.

"Tia called close to five. I had invited her over for dinner and wine. She was feeling a little down . . ." Cassidy hesitated.

Jack rolled one hand to urge her on.

"Well, anyway, I didn't think she should be alone, but she said she was going to take Dozer for another run and wear herself out, then take a hot soak, and go to bed."

"She called from the build site."

"Yes. Shouldn't we call the police, Jack?"

Jack lifted Dozer and set him on the floor. "You do that while I head to the site and talk to the guards. It's too soon for them to file a formal missing persons report, but call anyway."

He let himself out without waiting for an answer and strapped Dozer into the passenger seat of the SUV. Dozer licked the side of Jack's face. "We'll find her," Jack said again. "I promise."

He wished he'd taken the time to change out of his suit pants and dress shoes while he'd been at the house, but he didn't want to waste the time to go back now. Tia was in trouble, and something told him time was of the essence.

CHAPTER 32

TIA CONTINUED to struggle with the door hinge. It was her only hope of escape. But the pin stubbornly refused to respond to her efforts. She wiggled it and leaned her back against the door, hoping to ease any pressure on the hinge.

Finally, she was rewarded with a slight upward movement. Elated, Tia kept working the pin free from the hinge in excruciatingly small increments. Her fingertips burned from the effort.

She wanted to shout out her victory when she gave a final pull and the pin fell to the floor. She toed it against the wall in case she needed it later and lifted her arms toward the middle hinge. This one proved more difficult because of the angle at which she was forced to hold her arms.

By the time she had the second pin worked almost free she wanted to scream from the pain in her shoulders. As the pin lifted, her arms would go no higher. She could feel that the pin was more than halfway out of the hinge, but she was unable to pull it free, even standing on her toes.

Tia dropped her hands and rolled her shoulders as best she could to ease the pain. She turned and stared at the pin with disgust. Now what? She had only one option.

Ignoring the decades of disgusting microbes that had gathered on the pin's head, she mashed her face against the frame, grabbed it with her teeth, and pulled. It took several tries, but eventually the pin joined the other one on the floor.

Tia did a very short victory jig, then stared at the third hinge. There was no way for her to reach it.

She would work with what she had.

She pressed her ear to the door again and listened. Heard nothing. Pressed her eye to the keyhole. Nothing had changed. If anything the light had faded some. She had no idea what time it was, but night must be falling.

She took several deep breaths to prepare herself. Her kidnapper could still be in the building but she had to risk the noise.

Tia stepped back from the door and kicked it hard. The door shuddered. She kicked at it again and again, until she could barely lift her right leg.

"Come on, you bastard, open for me."

She rested a moment and decided to change tactics. Instead of kicking the door near the hinges, she aimed for the keyhole with her left leg. The door shuddered like before, but this time the hinges sprang slightly apart. Encouraged, Tia took a deep breath and kicked with everything she had.

The two lower hinges moved apart and the lower inner edge of the door popped slightly away from the frame. Tia turned her back to the door, grabbed the newly freed edge with her hands, and pulled until she heard wood splinter and she had a space large enough to squeeze through.

Sobbing with relief, Tia took a minute to search this new room for something she could use to cut the tie holding her hands. She found an old Gatorade bottle and whacked it against the door frame. Her first try failed. Her second try she swung harder and was rewarded with the sound of breaking glass.

She sank to her knees and felt for the neck of the broken bottle. She caught a sharp edge first and cut her finger. Turning her head, she located the piece she wanted and after several failed attempts grabbed onto it.

Now for the tricky part. Moving slowly, she slid her fingers to the broken edge of the piece and carefully pressed the neck between her boot heels so the broken edge stood upright.

But when she tried to rub the plastic zip tie against the bottle, the bottle slipped from her heels and rolled to the floor. Two more tries yielded the same result.

"Hey! How the hell did you get out?"

Tia's head whipped around. She had been so focused on freeing herself she'd forgotten to listen for her captor's return. Stupid!

The tattooed man crossed the room in three long strides and punched Tia in the face. Sharp pain exploded across her right cheekbone. She lost her balance and fell on her bruised shoulder. Hissing from the pain, she grabbed blindly for the broken bottle but her captor kicked it out of her reach.

"Stupid bitch, you're more trouble than you're worth. I should just kill you now and leave you here."

Tia said nothing. She watched the snake's tongue seem to flick across the man's cheek as he worked his jaw and suppressed a shudder.

The man stalked across the room, then back, swearing. He pulled his foot back and kicked her right hip.

Tia bit her bottom lip to keep from crying out. Somehow she knew that any reaction would spur him on.

The man glared down at her, his breathing fast and heavy. He swore again and left the room, returning a moment later with another zip tie which he used to secure Tia's ankles.

She kicked out at him but her aim was off and her boot

glanced off his calf. He grabbed her foot and twisted so hard she thought her ankle would break.

"That oughtta hold ya," he said, tightening the tie on Tia's ankles so they were pressed tightly together. He straightened, grabbed her arm, and dragged her back into the room from which she had worked so hard to escape. Before leaving her he whipped off the filthy kerchief he wore around his neck and gagged her with it.

"Stay put and maybe you'll live through this. Or maybe you won't. I honestly don't care one way or another, long as I get paid."

Tia closed her eyes and willed Jack to find her.

JACK'S first stop after leaving Cassidy's was the build site. He pulled up to the closed and locked gate and laid on his horn, then jumped out of the vehicle.

"Wait here, Dozer. I'll be right back." The dog barked once and strained against the seat belt.

"No," Jack said more firmly. "Stay." He lowered the window for the dog then walked to the gate and scanned the lot. There was no sign of Tia's truck and only one guard car belonging to Mark. Where was Roland?

Mark came toward him, lifting a hand in greeting. "Mr. Orion. What brings you here?"

"I'm looking for Tia," Jack answered. "Did you see her when you came on shift?"

Mark nodded. "Sure, sure. She was here. Miles had to leave early for something so she waited for us."

"Us?" Jack pointed toward Mark's car. "I don't see Roland's vehicle."

"I meant me." Mark's eyes shifted toward Jack's car. He stiffened when he saw Dozer. "How'd you end up with Dozer? I thought he never left the boss lady's side."

Dozer began to bark and struggle against the seatbelt.

"Long story. Where's Roland?"

Mark couldn't seem to pull his attention away from Dozer. "Roland called me right before shift and said he was too sick to drag his sorry ass in here. Tia really ought to hire herself another professional, if you ask me. As you can see, I'm on my own."

"Thanks." Jack turned and headed back to the SUV. "Easy boy. We're going to find her, I promise."

Mark was still standing at the gate when he drove away.

Jack already knew where Roland lived from when someone had intentionally given him a flat tire. He headed for the guard's apartment on Portland's west end near the sprawling Maine Medical Center.

He took Dozer with him this time, commanding the pup to heel as he climbed to the third floor in Roland's building. It was a decent place, an older six unit building with two apartments to a floor. The foyer was clean and well lit and even had a green plant stuck in the corner.

It took several bangs on Roland's door before he heard movement within.

"Just a minute. I'm coming."

Roland opened the door. He wore a set of University of Maine sweats and looked like hell. Freckles stood out on his pasty white face and his dark blond hair stood up in tufts. He leaned heavily against the door.

"Mr. Orion. Why are you here? And Dozer. Hey, boy."

"I heard you were sick, thought I'd better check it out," Jack said smoothly. God, the kid really was sick. He looked like he could barely stand. "Make sure you drink plenty of fluids and get back to bed."

"My mom said the same thing when I called her." Roland started to close the door, hesitated. "Is Miss Tia all right?"

Jack took a big step back toward Roland. "What makes you ask that?" he demanded.

Roland pointed at Dozer. "You have her dog. Dozer never leaves Miss Tia's side. He's about as devoted as a pet can get. Wish I had me a dog like that," he added wistfully.

Jack stood thinking for a minute. "Roland, when did you get sick?"

"About an hour before my shift. Mark and I grabbed dinner at the Mexican place down on St. John and I was feeling pretty crummy by the time we left. I figured I ate something bad. I'll never eat there again. Been hanging on the toilet since I got home. Why?"

Jack shook his head. "No reason. Just hoping it isn't contagious. I have to go." He turned and ran down the stairs and crashed out the front door.

That bastard Mark knew something. Jack was willing to bet that Mark had put something into Roland's food to make him ill. And Dozer had known. The dog had tried to tell him if he'd only paid attention.

Mark was going to tell Jack what was going on and then Jack was going to kill him.

He strapped Dozer back in his seat and headed back to the build site, but when he got there he saw that Mark's red Dodge Ram was gone.

Jack slapped his steering wheel. "Dammit." Now what? "Think, Jack. You need to think. Tia's life might depend on you." Dozer looked at him and whined.

An icy ball of fear churned in Jack's belly. If Garapolo was behind Tia's disappearance she might never be found. Unfortunately he didn't have any proof that Garapolo was involved. If he went bursting into a mob-connected guy's restaurant flinging accusations he might not walk out again.

He'd save Garapolo as a last resort.

Inspiration struck. It was time to track down Tia's assistant Miles and find out what the man knew. Unfortunately he didn't have Miles's phone number, but he'd bet that Ashley had it somewhere in her files on Tia's project. Ashley was very thorough and always kept everything.

He whipped out his phone as he headed toward his office and dialed Ashley's number. She answered after the third ring.

"Hello? Jack? I thought you were out with Miss Albrecht tonight."

"Ashley, I need Miles Angsley's phone number. Is it in the Bayside file?" There was several seconds of silence on the line. "Ashley? You still there?"

"What do you need Miles's number for?"

Jack heard the strain in Ashley's voice and other voices around her. "Where are you?" he asked.

Ashley sighed. "On a dinner cruise. . . with Miles."

Jack had just pulled into his parking space at the office. He pulled back out again. The island ferry wharf was nearby. "When do you dock?"

"In about twenty minutes. What's this about, Jack?"

Jack didn't bother to answer her question. "I'll meet you on the dock." He hung up and headed for the Casco Bay Lines parking lot.

Few cars used the lot at this hour. The last ferry run for island commuters had just left and this time of night most of the tourists used the parking garages conveniently located near the bars and restaurants they liked to frequent. Even the seagulls who filled the waterfront's sky during the day looking for dropped food had gone to their roosts for the night.

Jack breathed in the familiar smells of salt, creosote, and tar. Small waves lapped softly at the edges of the wharf. Three blasts from the dinner cruise ferry's horn rent the air as it slowed on its approach.

He was pacing back and forth by the time Ashley and Miles came down the ferry's ramp. Miles held Ashley's hand and looked none too pleased to see Jack waiting for them.

"What's this about, Orion? Ashley is entitled to a private life outside your office. She isn't at your beck and call twenty-four seven."

Apparently Ashley hadn't told her date that Jack was looking for him. He wondered why not, then dismissed it.

"Tia's missing. When did you see her last?"

Miles stopped. Several people jostled into him and Ashley before Jack led them back to the parking lot, out of the way of the departing passengers.

"Missing?" Miles narrowed his eyes at Jack. "What did you do to Tia anyway? She barely talks and she's been working harder than anyone else on the site for the last day or two. She always works hard, but not to the point where I can see that she's exhausting herself."

Jack set his jaw and restrained himself from grabbing Miles by the throat. "*When* did you last talk with Tia, Miles? I'm about at the end of my rope here."

Miles lifted his chin. "She's probably avoiding you. Ever think about that?"

Jack glared at Tia's assistant foreman. He itched to smash Miles on that lifted chin but he knew it would get him nowhere. He walked over to his SUV instead and let Dozer out.

"Dozer?" Miles lost his cockiness. "Tia wouldn't go any place without Dozer. What's going on?"

"When did you leave the build site?" asked Jack, holding Dozer's collar so the dog wouldn't bother the people heading to their cars.

"About five. I usually stay until the night guards show up but Ashley and I had a date for the dinner cruise so Tia waited for them instead. What do they say?"

"Roland is home sick. And before you ask, yes, he's really sick. I stopped by his apartment to check."

"And Mark?" Miles looked worried now.

"Mark was alone at the build site when I stopped by the first time. I went back after speaking with Roland and he was gone."

"Gone? I don't understand," Miles said. "How'd you end up with Dozer?"

"Someone found him wandering a street near the site. Tia's truck hasn't been found yet." A group of young men whooped and laughed on the street, most likely headed for a waterfront bar. Their gaiety felt out of place when the most important person in Jack's world was missing and in danger.

"Who knew you were going on the dinner cruise tonight?" he asked Miles suddenly.

Miles wagged his head side to side and frowned. "I don't know. Tia, naturally. Maybe one or two of the guys at work. A couple of the guys were interested because they want to impress their wives, you know?"

"Not them." Jack shook his head. "It wasn't them. Who else?"

"No one. I don't have roommates."

Ashley cleared her throat. Her face looked pale under the parking lot lights.

Jack turned to look at her. His gut clenched. "Who did you tell, Ashley?" he asked softly. His admin assistant looked miserable. And then he knew. "Your brother?"

Ashley nodded. "Trevor–Trevor suggested the cruise to me and told me to invite Miles."

Jack fought to keep his temper in check. "And the night Tia was attacked at the site? Did Trevor know she'd be there alone then?"

Tears leaked from Ashley's eyes. Miles looked at her in horror and dropped her hand. He took a step away from her. "You've been using me so your brother–Trevor, is it?–can get to my boss?" He shook his head. "I can't believe how stupid I've been."

"Never mind that." Jack didn't have time for Miles's relationship problems. "Where is your brother now, Ashley? *Tell me.*"

"I–I don't know. He's been staying with me the last few weeks but he wasn't at my apartment when I dressed for our date. He promised that nothing bad would happen to her. He was . . . just doing a friend a favor and getting paid well for it."

She turned to Miles and held her hands out toward him. "Please let me explain, Miles."

Miles held his palms up. "I can't talk to you right now. You'll have to call a cab. I need to help Jack find Tia."

"No." Jack grabbed Ashley's arm. "We're going to your place so I can search your brother's things. With luck I'll find something that will tell me where he's holding Tia."

Jack put Dozer in the back of the SUV. Miles took Dozer's place and Ashley sat alone in the back. Tomorrow Jack would fire her. If he found Tia.

If he hadn't found Tia by tomorrow then he was hauling Ashley's ass down to the police station and having her charged with conspiracy to commit a kidnapping.

He put the SUV in gear and peeled out of the ferry parking lot.

CHAPTER 34

TIA LAY against the back wall of the small room and took stock of her situation. Her ankles, shoulders, and hands ached and her hip throbbed where Snakeman had kicked her. The gag tasted vile and hurt the corners of her mouth.

Her situation had definitely deteriorated.

Light no longer filtered through the crack above the plywood over the window. It had to be after nine at least, maybe later. When would she be missed?

Was Jack still enjoying his dinner with the lovely Tamara? Or had they moved on to a cozy evening together in bed? What if Jack didn't go back to the house?

Tamara Albrecht would never find herself in a situation like this, Tia thought with disgust.

Snakeman had ripped the door from its last hinge and tossed it aside before dragging Tia back into her prison room. Unable to catch her balance with her ankles tied together, she had rolled and landed where she now lay.

Her captor sat in the other room staring intently at his phone. He seemed to be waiting for something. The battery powered camp lantern he had lit in the other room cast his grotesque shadow against the far wall–a creepy twin to a creepy man. She knew he couldn't see her as the dim light didn't reach into her small space.

Where were her brothers when she needed them? Now would be a good time to make up for all those times they had tormented her when she was a young teenaged girl. Would she ever see her family again? Tia blinked back the tears that sprang to her eyes.

She would not cry. Crying wouldn't help her out of this situation.

She knew that Snakeman couldn't let her live. His tattoos made him too easy to identify. What was his plan? How would he kill her? And what was he waiting for?

Tia turned the situation over in her mind. Snakeman had obviously been hired to kidnap her. Was Mark in on it or had her kidnapper subdued him? She couldn't remember the sequence of events–not exactly. She remembered Mark telling her that Roland had called him and told him he was ill. Mark had hired Snakeman to fill in for Roland for the night.

How did they know each other?

She had put Dozer into her truck. Dozer! Oh, her poor pup must be frantic. Her breath hitched. What if they had killed Dozer after grabbing her?

This time she couldn't prevent the tears from falling. She closed her eyes and willed Dozer to be alive. Cassidy would take him if Tia didn't return. Even Jack–but no, somehow she couldn't picture Tamara as a dog person unless it was one of those little teacup-sized creatures.

Tia drifted, then opened her eyes. Despite her discomfort she must have dozed. The camp light still burned in the other room but she could no longer see her captor. He must have left the room while she slept.

He had left the light burning though. He wouldn't be away for long.

She tried to rub her nose on her shoulder but couldn't reach it. She pulled her knees to her chest and rubbed her tear-stained face on them instead. She had to pull herself together. No one knew where she was. No one was coming to save her. It was up to her to save herself.

She took several deep breaths, using the nasty smells of kitty litter and urine and stale beer to wake her up. Shifting her body so she could see more of the other room, she spied light glinting off glass near the doorway.

The broken bottle! If she could grab it and bring it back into the room she could work on her restraints.

Pressing her feet against the wall, she straightened her legs. The movement brought her halfway to the doorway, but left her with nothing to press against so she could move further.

She pulled her knees up and used her bound feet to wiggle her body around until she could roll toward the door. A sound from the other room stilled her. She waited, and several moments later heard it again. She searched what she could see of the room and saw some of the trash shift.

Oh lord, rats. If there were enough of them they would attack her. She fought down a surge of panic. *Forget them, Tia. Do what you have to do.*

Tia rolled toward the door as fast as she could, grunting from the pain in her hip and shoulders. Not caring whether she made noise or not, she kicked and maneuvered until she could grasp the broken glass. Luck was with her finally—it was the top half of the bottle.

She couldn't roll back and hang onto the bottle piece at the same time so she inch-wormed her way to the back wall and out of sight of the doorway and went to work.

Drawing her feet up behind her as high as she could, she wedged the bottle piece between her boots. The tie holding her ankles together worked to her advantage now, holding her boots with the glass firmly in place even when she pressed down on it.

Spreading her hands as far apart as possible–which wasn't far at all–Tia missed the tie her first few tries and caught her wrists instead. She refused to give up, despite her nicked and bleeding fingers and the warm trickle of blood running down her hands from her wrists.

The plastic tie was amazingly strong. She sawed back and forth across the bottle top's jagged edge until she heard Snakeman return to the other room. She stilled when he walked toward her.

Of course. She had moved too far to the side of the room and he could no longer see her from where he sat.

He stood in the doorway, a lean, sinewy dark shape with a shaved skull, but he said nothing until he turned away.

"She's fine. Trussed up like a turkey–she ain't going anywhere. Did you get my money?"

Snakeman wasn't alone! Tia pressed harder against the edge of the glass and sawed as quickly as she could.

"Yeah, I have your cut. You're leaving town tonight, right?"

Tia stilled again. She knew that voice. It was . . . Mark, the night guard. He was in on her kidnapping. She wanted to yell at him that he was a fool and ask him what he'd done with her dog, but fortunately the gag prevented her from speaking.

"Yeah, I'm leaving," Snakeman answered. "Headed down the pike to Boston. I'll catch a flight out of Logan. You?"

"Oh, yeah, I'm on my way now. Orion came looking for her. I hightailed it as soon as he left the site. Picked up our payoff and came straight here. The Boss had the kitchen throw in a couple meatball subs if you're hungry."

"Great. I'm starved. We'll eat while we divide the money."

The smell of spicy tomato sauce and meatballs wafted into the small back room. Tia listened, barely daring to breathe. Orion had been looking for her? The knowledge gave her fresh hope that she might survive after all.

She heard the two men counting and worked harder at the tie binding her hands. Finally it snapped free and she almost groaned aloud with relief. The nerves in her hands and arms tingled with the fresh flow of blood. She stretched and massaged her cramped fingers, then pulled the piece of bottle free from where it was still wedged between her boots and went to work on the tie binding her ankles.

The ankle tie gave way much faster because she was able to get a better grip on the broken glass and a better angle to work at the tie. The gag was tied too tight to cut it free and she couldn't loosen the knot. She left it for later.

Now what? She had a better chance at escaping this night-mare with her feet and hands free, but there were still the two men to deal with. She couldn't just run by them—she had no idea of the layout of the building they were holding her in and they'd be on her before she made it out of the other room.

The window was still out of the question. Maybe go up through the ceiling? She eyed the distance. Old buildings tended to have eight-to-ten foot ceilings and this one was no exception. She'd never reach it without something to stand on.

"It's all here," she heard Mark say, his voice filled with satis-faction. "Hundred thou for you and a hundred thou for me."

She heard the two men get to their feet.

"Been a pleasure doing business with you, Trev." Mark's chuckle turned to a gurgle. "What are you—"

"Oh yeah, been a real pleasure, man. Only thing is, I'm going to need the whole two hundred thousand for myself. Running gets expensive. Sorry, pal."

A body thumped on the floor.

Tia's heart stuttered in her chest. Had she just heard Snakeman murder Mark? And what did that mean for her?

She stood and shook out her legs, then stepped silently to the side of the open doorway. She still held the broken glass. It was the only weapon she had.

Her toe hit one of the hinge pins she had dropped and it clunked lightly against the wall. She froze. Damn, she had forgotten about the pins. Had Snakeman heard it?

She waited for several long breaths but her kidnapper paid the sound no attention. She risked a quick look and saw that he was stripping Mark's body of valuables. A long, thin knife lay on the floor beside him. Blood covered the blade and Mark's front.

Tia bent and quickly picked up the two hinge pins. Making a fist with her left hand, she jammed the pins in her curled fingers so they stuck out several inches beyond the edge of her hand. Now she had two weapons. They weren't much against a knife, but they were better than her bare hands.

She stood against the wall just beyond the edge of the doorway and waited.

CHAPTER 35

JACK'S SEARCH of Ashley's brother's room had yielded little. Much to Ashley's surprise, her brother had cleaned out his personal effects, leaving only fast food bags and empty beer cans.

Trevor Hayes was on the run, or soon would be. Jack took the time to look through the trash, despite his need to get out there and search for Tia. He felt the edges of panic pushing at his mind. She could be anywhere in the Greater Portland area. Or outside the city. Unfortunately there was no convenient piece of paper with an address pointing him to Tia's whereabouts.

Miles and Dozer watched him from the doorway. Miles hadn't spoken to Ashley since they'd left the Casco Bay Lines parking lot. Ashely had withdrawn to her living room couch after showing Jack to her brother's room.

"Nothing," Jack said in disgust, balling up the last sandwich wrapper and tossing it to the floor. Dozer walked into the room and sniffed at the balled up paper.

Miles entered the room and picked up a sandwich shop bag, smoothing it out so the name showed clearly. He held it out to Jack. "This might be out in left field, but Maggie's Sandwich Shop is down by the west end railroad tracks, near the old strip mall. What business would Trevor Hayes have down there, I wonder?"

Jack shrugged, dismissing the question. "How should I know? The slimeball could be up to anything."

Miles shook the bag at Jack. "No, Jack, listen. There's a row of four or five condemned apartment buildings built in the forties near the river end of St. John street. That whole stretch has been for sale for a couple of years now. So far nobody's been interested in the land because it's practically on top of the tracks and it's a case of out of sight, out of mind. It isn't really suited for anything."

"How do *you* know about it?" Jack frowned at the bag in Miles' hand. A small kernel of hope began to grow in his chest.

"Tia had an idea for the land if she didn't get the Bayside project. We walked it together last year. There were squatters living in the old apartment buildings even though they're boarded up. Maggie's isn't far from there."

Jack snatched the sandwich bag from Miles' hand. "It's the best lead we have. Good catch, Miles."

He headed out to the living room and planted himself in front of Ashley. She lifted her face from her hands and looked at him. Her eyes were filled with misery, her shoulders slumped.

"You're going to fire me, aren't you?"

"Possibly. Probably. What kind of car does your brother drive?"

"A green Hundai sedan. I don't know the model. Why?"

Jack didn't answer, he was already headed out the apartment door with Miles and Dozer on his heels.

Ten minutes later, with Miles directing him, Jack pulled his SUV onto the edge of a dry, grassy patch on the far side of a row of dilapidated apartment buildings. A steep hill backed the apartments. Lights from the sprawling Maine Medical campus shone from the far left of the hilltop. Unseen but directly above, sat the elegant, stately homes of the Western Promenade.

Railroad tracks ran on the opposite side of the road, between the road and the tidal Fore River. The buildings would have looked out over the river and possibly even had their own docks when they were first built. It was a strange place to invest in apartments, but the narrow strip of land had most likely been cheap and Portland had begun its long growth spurt and needed affordable housing.

Jack turned off the SUV's interior light before they both climbed out and quietly shut the doors. He held the heavy Mag flashlight he kept in the vehicle in one hand and Dozer's collar in the other. The stench of exposed mud flats filled the air. The tide was out.

"Let's walk around the back first," he whispered. Miles nodded and the men made their way to the back of the buildings.

Jack released his hold on Dozer's collar so the dog could pick his way through the obstacle course of discarded appliances, rusty swingsets, and barbecue grills. He hoped they didn't run into broken glass—he didn't want to have to explain to Tia how Dozer's paws got cut up.

No sound came from inside the first or second building, and no light showed anywhere. Jack checked both back doors and found them padlocked. If squatters were using those two buildings they were most likely climbing in through a broken window.

He walked around both buildings, checking the basements for a way in. Sure enough, someone had kicked in the plywood covering the small cellar window on the second building's back side.

It was a risk not to check the buildings out more thoroughly, but he didn't think Tia's kidnapper would want to haul her through a small window.

Jack started for the third building but Miles gave a soft

whistle and pointed down the dark, narrow space between the third and fourth buildings.

Jack joined him and looked. A small dark sedan and a big red truck filled the space. A half fallen wooden fence hid them from the street.

Dozer shot away from Jack and up the back steps of the third building and scratched at the door. Jack followed more slowly, checking each step to make sure it would bear his weight. His heart skipped a beat when he saw that the padlock on the back door had been cut and hung loose.

Taking a deep breath, Jack reached for the door handle, but drew back.

"What's wrong?" Miles hissed. "They're in there."

Jack wished now that he'd left Dozer in the SUV. What if the pup went charging in after Tia and got her hurt? Her kidnappers could grab her and use her as a shield. They might even have a gun.

"Dozer," he mouthed, pointing to the dog.

Miles frowned, then his expression cleared. He climbed the steps and grabbed Dozer's collar. "I've got him. Go," he said quietly.

JACK REACHED for the door handle again and pushed slowly, praying that it wouldn't squeak, but the door was slightly swollen and scraped across the old linoleum floor. He pushed until he had created a space wide enough to squeeze through, then waited, his ears straining to hear the slightest noise. He heard nothing but his own breathing.

He waited several minutes longer to be sure, minutes that felt like hours, then stepped carefully inside the apartment. Miles stayed on the back step with Dozer.

The heavy, moldy smell of damp and rotting plaster assailed Jack's nose. Placing his fingers over the lens of the flashlight so only a small amount of light leaked through, he flashed it briefly around the space.

The back door opened directly into the apartment's kitchen. There were gaping holes where appliances once stood. The copper plumbing had been ripped out and probably sold by scavengers. Trash and chunks of fallen plaster littered the cracked and faded linoleum floor.

All the windows were boarded with plywood. There was no furniture and no sign of Tia.

Behind him Dozer whined. Jack realized he needed to move fast before Dozer alerted the kidnappers to their presence. He stepped to the hallway leading from the kitchen and stopped. A dim light glowed from the second doorway on the left side of the hall. Squatters? Or the kidnappers?

He trusted Dozer. Tia was in here somewhere.

The coppery, metallic scent of fresh blood reached him, sending a chill of apprehension down Jack's spine. Please let him not be too late.

He made his way as quietly and quickly as he could down the hall, testing each step for rotten boards. When he reached the lighted doorway he stopped again to listen.

The smell of blood grew stronger. Jack wanted to race into the room but knew that was not the right way to approach two dangerous men. Considering the blood, at least one of them was armed.

He paused. Who was bleeding? It took a fair amount of blood to scent the air. Had there been a falling out between Mark and Ashley's brother?

The sound of a zipper came from the room, followed by a soft chuckle.

"I'm sorry things have to end this way." A male voice.

"But witnesses, you know," the voice continued. "I can't take a chance on just leaving you here to die. Can't have you going to the cops if some squatter finds you and lets you go."

Jack couldn't wait any longer. He stepped to the doorway and saw a bald-headed man step through another doorway on the opposite side of the room. A battery-powered camp lantern lit a grisly scene. Mark lay on his back, his front soaked in blood, his eyes staring at nothing.

Before Jack could attack the kidnapper, Tia came flying at the bald man from out of the darkness, slashing at him with both her fists.

The bald man screamed in anger then lifted a long blade to slash at her.

Dozer came charging past Jack and leaped onto the bald man's back with a growl that raised the hairs on the back of Jack's neck.

The kidnapper fell to his face. Tia stomped hard on his hand and kicked the knife away, then aimed her boot at the man's ribs and kicked him again.

"Tia!"

Jack ran forward and jerked the man's hands behind him, planting a foot firmly in his back. "Stay where you are, Mr. Hayes," he warned. "It wouldn't take much of an excuse for me to kill you."

He looked up at Tia—his beautiful Tia—and winced. She had another black eye. Her hands were covered with blood. She held half of a broken bottle in one and something metal in the other. He tried to speak past the hard lump filling his throat.

She was breathing hard through a filthy gag, her green eyes wild and angry. Suddenly she tossed away her weapons, dropped to her knees, and pulled Dozer to her, burying her face in his neck.

Miles joined them and handed Jack a couple zip ties. "Found these in the scumbag's duffle. Along with Mark's watch and wallet and a big pile of money."

Jack secured Ashley's brother and stood. He wasn't sure what to do. Tia hadn't turned to him, she'd reached for her dog for comfort.

Obviously she was unaware of how he felt about her. And that was his fault. Hadn't he told her he was marrying Tamara?

"Call the police," Jack told Miles.

He grabbed Tia gently by the shoulders and pulled her to her feet. "Let me get that gag off you, sweetheart," he said.

Had she heard right? Did Orion just call her sweetheart? She couldn't believe that he had found her. He should be having dinner, or sex, or *something* with Tamara, but he was here, with her instead. And he had called her sweetheart. Did that mean he cared?

Tia turned her back so Orion could untie the gag but the knot defeated him. In the end he took the pocket knife he always carried–even in his dress slacks–and cut it off. She wanted to laugh about the knife, but knew that the urge was just a hysteric reaction and she needed to get a grip on herself.

Now that her ordeal was over, violent tremors shook Tia's body and her teeth chattered. Jack turned her and gathered her into his arms, holding her close. He felt big and solid and warm and safe and she couldn't stop the tears that flowed down her cheeks.

"My Tia." He murmured her name over and over and softly stroked her hair. "I thought I'd lost you. I couldn't bear it."

A siren approached the house and cut off.

"I'll guide them in," Miles said, and left them alone.

"Tia." Jack lifted her chin so he could look into her face. "I've been an idiot. I love you. I think I fell in love with you that first day when you accused me of leaving a cooler filled with rotten fish on your porch."

He brushed his lips lightly over hers. "Do you think–what I want to know is, is there any chance you could learn to love me back? I want to marry you. I want to make a family with you. I need you, Tia. I'm a better man when I'm with you."

Dazed, Tia could only stare up into Orion's handsome face. He wanted to marry her? Her? Not Tamara?

"What–" The word came out as a rusty whisper. She tried again. "What about Tamara?"

"Tamara can find another business partner. I want a real wife, one who's warm and passionate and likes my cooking and isn't afraid to challenge me. I want you, Tia. Please. Could you find it in your heart to love me? Will you marry me?"

Tia placed bloodied fingers on Orion's cheek. "Yes," she whispered. "I'll marry you. I love you, Orion."

Jack groaned and kissed her. He lifted his head as two officers came into the room with Miles. "Do you think you could call me Jack?" he whispered.

A teasing light came into Tia's eyes. "Nope. You'll always be Orion to me."

"I'll take it." Jack kissed the tip of her nose and turned to face the others.

CHAPTER 37

Five Years Later

"Phoebe, sweetheart, don't pull Dozer's ears. You'll hurt him." Jack bent and swung the toddler into the air and caught her. She laughed, her black curls bouncing around her head, her beautiful green eyes wide and smiling. He rubbed his nose against hers and breathed in the clean scent of his daughter.

The Realis and the Orions were having their bi-monthly, Sunday afternoon get-together at Cassidy and Leonard's house, taking advantage of the beautiful fall day with a barbecue.

The horror of Tia's kidnapping and Mark's murder had faded with the intervening years. Trevor Hayes was serving a life term in prison, thanks to Tia's testimony against him.

Hayes fingered Garapolo, who had been found floating in the bay, victim of a suspected but unproven murder. Rumors claimed he had owed large sums of money to the wrong people. Jack's only regret was that Garapolo wasn't suffering in prison along with Hayes.

The Bayside project was nearly finished and already proving

to be a vibrant destination spot filled with happy tenants. Tia's next project sat on her drawing board–she had purchased the condemned buildings where she'd been held captive and planned to replace them with a public park geared especially for children.

"More, Dada," Phoebe said, patting her father's cheeks with pudgy little hands. "Up."

Jack tossed her two more times, laughing as she screeched with glee.

"Uh, Jack, that might not be such a good idea considering she just ate a big bowl of your wife's potato salad," Leonard pointed out. He shut down the lid of the latest grill Cassidy and the boys had given him for Father's Day and grabbed a beer from the cooler.

"Give her to me, Jack." Cassidy stepped up to him and held out her arms. "I never get enough cuddle time with our little girl. The boys are wonderful, but they don't cuddle."

Jack's daughter wrapped her arms around Auntie Cassie's neck and started babbling at her.

"Dad! Dad!" Jack's four year old son ran toward him with Dozer on his heels. Blonde and blue-eyed like his father, Damon already showed signs of inheriting his father's height and build.

"Dad! Griffin and Carter said I can play catch with them." Cassidy and Leonard's youngest son, nine year old Griffin, was Damon's hero. He shadowed the older boy whenever the families got together. Fortunately Griffin had a friendly, easy nature and didn't mind a short tagalong.

Damon grabbed Jack's hand and tugged. "You can play too. Griffin said. Come on."

"In a minute, son. I want to see if your mother needs anything, then I'll join you."

Damon jumped off the deck. "He said he's going to play in a minute!" he shouted as he ran back to the other boys.

Jack shook his head and chuckled. Who knew children could

be so entertaining? He walked to the side of the Reali's large back deck where Tia lay stretched out in a chaise lounge and sat beside her.

"Do you need anything?" he asked, rubbing his hand on Tia's mounded abdomen. They were expecting the newest addition to their family in another month. He leaned down and kissed the woman who had changed his life. "More lemonade? Fizzy water?"

She smiled at him. "Actually, if you have the children I thought I'd waddle home and take a nap."

Neither her house on Munjoy Hill nor Jack's loft apartment had been large enough for a growing family plus houseguests, so they had sold them both and found a large place two streets over from Cassidy and Leonard, with an in-law apartment for when her family members came to stay, which was fairly often now that there were grandchildren to spoil.

Tia placed a hand over Jack's on her very pregnant belly. "This one seems to sap more energy than the first two."

"Maybe that's because you're going to have twins." Cassie plopped down on the chaise next to Tia's and tried to settled Phoebe on her lap, but the little girl wriggled down and ran after the boys. "Trust me. I can tell. There are two in there," she said, pointing to Tia's belly with a wide smile.

Tia laughed and shook her head. "Mom would be ecstatic."

"When did Mom say they were going to arrive?" Jack asked. His in-laws had welcomed him into the family with open hearts. After learning that Jack had been orphaned as a young boy and had no family, Tia's mother had insisted that he call her Mom.

Tia's father still preferred to be called Zeus—or Sir—but he treated Jack like one of his own sons, which meant that he was as stern and demanding of Jack as he was of Tia's brothers.

Jack couldn't be happier. Finally, after a lifetime of being alone in the world, he had a family. Sisters-in-law and brothers and nieces and nephews and aunts and uncles. After five years he still felt a little overwhelmed to have found so much.

Marrying Artemis Smith had been the smartest move he'd ever made. And to think it all came about because of a cooler full of rotten fish and the trouble that followed.

I'm glad you found this book out of the millions available. If you'd like to know when I release a new book instead of leaving it to chance you can sign up for my newsletter. You can also see what I'm working on or even send me an email– all through my website, CharleyMarshBooks.

Turn the page for the first chapter of Andromeda, the fourth book in the Romancing a God series.

ANDROMEDA

ROMANCING A GOD SERIES

CHARLEY MARSH

CHAPTER 1

Andromeda White stared blindly at the spreadsheet numbers on her screen and sighed. It was nearly six on a Friday night. Yet another Friday evening that saw her toiling alone on the seventh floor of the Cephus White Building while her co-workers headed off to have drinks with friends or home to share dinner with waiting families.

Not that she could have gone with them even if someone had thought to invite her. Tonight she had to attend yet another stuffy event with her parents.

The Cephus White Sports gala was always held the third Friday evening in June and that meant that tonight she had to paste on a smile and make friendly with people she mostly saw only once a year–at the gala–as well as total strangers. Never an easy thing for someone who tripped over her own tongue with shyness.

Whoever had decreed these modern business-social affairs as worthy of the term "gala" had been way off base. Gala came from the French "gale" which meant rejoice. As far as Andi could tell there was no rejoicing at these events, only elbow rubbing and too many people trying to impress one another.

Unfortunately they also tried to impress her because they thought she'd put in a good word for them with her father. Which meant she'd be forced to talk when she'd much rather stand quietly off to the side and observe. She'd learned at an early age that people who were nice to her usually wanted something.

She scowled at the dress bag hanging on the back of her office door. It had arrived several hours ago by special courier, along with a note from her mother informing Andi that she had just the earrings and necklace to go with it and her parents would pick her up at her condo at seven-thirty.

The knowledge that she would once again be paraded in front of people like a prized bull settled like a stone around Andi's heart.

She closed the spreadsheet, shut down her computer, and leaned back in her chair to ponder her life. Her office was small and had no window and was a step up from the rows of gray-blue cubicles that filled the large space outside her door. Gray carpet covered the floor. Two hard-backed oak chairs and her desk, a large gray metal affair with zero personality and not a smidgeon of beauty, filled the space.

She'd rather have a cubicle if it meant a few of the other workers would accept her. Invite her to have an after work drink with them. Or share a pizza. She liked pizza a lot. She certainly preferred it to the fancy tidbits she'd be served at the gala.

Andi stretched her long body with a heavy sigh. Maybe this one would be different. Maybe the servers would offer trays of pizza bites. She smiled at the thought. Her mother would consider such fare "common" and not suitably impressive. She loved her mother but the woman was an undeniable snob.

Her co-workers would think she was nuts to prefer a glass of wine in a bar with friends over a fancy dress gala event. Maybe they'd be right. Maybe she had been spoiled by too many business social affairs. Her parents started dragging her to them

when she turned sixteen in the hopes that she'd develop the rela-
tionships necessary to take over Cephus White Sports when her
father retired.

She supposed the first time she'd attended an event with her
parents she must have been awed and excited. She couldn't
remember. Eight years had passed since that first event and
there'd been too many since. The people were always the same,
the conversations about nothing.

All but one row of lights snapped off outside her office door.
The night watchman was making his rounds. He knew that Andi
was always the last to leave, especially at the end of the work
week and he left a row of lights on to guide her out. She heard
the elevator ding as the watchman headed back down and knew
she needed to leave, but remained seated.

She had argued against working for her father but he had
sabotaged any attempt she made at finding a job that she wanted
to do. She'd finally given up after being turned down for every
position she'd applied for, even entry level positions for the
simplest of jobs. Her father, Cepheus White, founder and president of Cephus White Sports, carried a lot of clout.

Andi slipped off her heels and pulled on her running shoes,
bagging each heel separately as her mother had trained her and
placed them in her leather tote bag.

Her mother would have a fit if she saw her only daughter
wearing black and red sneakers with a sage green linen suit.

The thought made Andi smile. Her mother Cass was a true
believer in always looking your best under any circumstances.
Andi had bought the ugly running shoes on a whim, probably to
defy her mother although she hadn't considered that at the
time.

She looked around her sparsly furnished office with a nagging
sense of disgust. While her mother had never worked–inside nor
outside the White home–Andi needed to work. Was it too much

to ask that the work be useful and make her feel that she was making the world better in some small way?

Running numbers for the marketing department on the floor above wasn't Andi's idea of making the world a better place. Her father had wanted to start her in a large corner office on the eighth floor but she had dug in her heels and refused. At least she'd won that skirmish, although she'd have preferred to work in a cubicle and not be singled out.

The seventh floor cubicles housed the Cephus White Sports customer service department, the guys and gals who took the phone orders and also keyed in orders from the company's extensive website. Andi tallied the number of daily orders taken for the various product lines and sent them to the sales reps on the eighth floor so they knew what to order more of and what wasn't selling.

It had taken less than half a day for the word to get around that she was the owner's daughter and any hope she had of making a few real friends who would like her for herself had died.

Andi shook off the old thoughts. It was time to head back to her condo to dress. Her parents would both fuss and lecture her on the importance of punctuality if she kept them waiting even a few mintes.

She snapped off her lights, pulled the dress bag from the hook on the door and hung it over her arm, picked up her leather tote, and closed and locked her office.

The center row of lights didn't quite reach the outer edges of the broad cubicle space but she wasn't afraid of the shadows. She had learned that shadows were her friend. A shy woman could melt into the background if she had shadows to hide in.

Her running shoes made no noise on the carpet. The single row of florescent lights buzzed faintly overhead. She could smell the remains of someone's curry lunch and too many varieties of perfume on the air.

Andi had never cared for perfume. In her opinion women tended to overspray. Perfumes made her sinuses swell and always seemed too artificial to her.

She understood why men and women wore heavy scents during England's Georgian era. Or was that the Edwardian era? Bathing was a rare occurence during both of those eras and people splashed on heavy scents to hide their body odor. These days there was no excuse for not bathing unless you were home-less or too ill.

She slapped the last light switches down as she went out the stairwell door. The seventh floor of the Cephus White building went dark behind her. The heavy fire door closed with a soft click and she was alone in the dim concrete stairwell. She began to run down the steps, her shoes making a soft shuffle on the smooth cement.

She counted the steps off as she went, a habit she had started and couldn't seem to drop. She counted them on the way up in the morning and again on the way down at the end of the day.

She never took the elevator, preferring to use the stairs for the exercise. She sat around too much during the day as it was, glued to a computer screen until black squiggles and lines danced in front of her eyes. She had never wanted to be a computer geek. It came easy to her—most intellectual things did—but that didn't mean she enjoyed it.

One hundred and eighty two steps brought her to the ground floor of her father's building where she exited the stairwell into the lobby.

"Good night, Gus." She waved to the night watchman.

"Good night, Miss Andromeda. I hope you have a date for tonight."

"Just with my parents, Gus. You know how it is. You're taken and I can't find anyone else to measure up." Gus's wrinkled face lit up with pleasure.

"Ahhh, Miss Andromeda. If only we'd met when I was a young man. I'd have swept you off your feet like you deserve. You have a good weekend now."

Andi stepped out into a mild spring evening. Turning left, she headed toward her riverside condo at a brisk pace, weaving in and out of knots of noisy college students and tourists heading for the many bars and restaurants in La Crosse's historic district.

She loved this section of the busy college town. Loved the fancy old brick buildings that had been built in response to several fires that had leveled the young city more than a century before. Modern store fronts now filled many of their ground floors but the upper floors, many made into apartments, retained their original bay windows and the intricate brickwork on the upper floors delighted her.

She turned down State Street and immediately cut through an alley that would take her to Main. The alley was wide enough for a single car to pass through and was remarkably clean even with the dumpsters for the burger pub and credit union that backed onto it. Most of La Crosse's alleys were clean and tended. It was one of the many reasons she loved it.

Andi was nearing the pub's dumpster when she spied the brown paper bag, a grocery store bag with the top folded over, set on top of a pile of green trash bags filling the pub's dumpster. The paper bag rattled and shook as she neared, making her pulse jump. Then it was still.

Suspecting that the bag was a college punk's idea of a prank, she looked up and down the alley to see if anyone was watching her but she was the only one there. She took a step closer to the bag and it shook again. The unpleasant stench of rotting garbage and wet cardboard filled her nose.

She didn't have time for pranks. She barely had time for a

shower if she was going to meet her parents on time. She turned away from the bag and it gave out a pitiful mew. Whirling back, Andi picked up the bag and carefully unfolded the top. A very angry kitten mewed up at her and leaped for the opening.

"Oh you poor thing," Andi crooned. She set down her tote and scooped inside the bag, wincing as the kitten's tiny claws dug into her wrist. It stared at her with wide golden eyes. It had calico fur, more black than orange or white, and it was spitting mad. It hissed at Andi to show its displeasure.

"I don't blame you, little one. What a rotten thing to do to a helpless animal." Obviously the kitten's callous owner had decided they didn't want her and had tossed her into the dumpster knowing full well it would be crushed in the garage truck's compressor.

"Well, I can't leave you here. You'll have to come home with me until I can take you to the shelter on Monday." She held the kitten against her chest and leaned down to grab her tote. Fortunately she only had a few more blocks to walk.

The kitten would need food. And a litter box. She could feed it a can of tuna tonight but the litter box was a problem she needed to solve right away.

You can find your copy of Andromeda at your favorite retailer here: https://books2read.com/Andromeda

ABOUT THE AUTHOR

Charley Marsh's curiosity drove her to climb mountains, canoe rivers, and explore caves and wilderness areas from Maine to California. She's been shot at, caught in a desert flash flood, and almost drowned off the Maine coast. Once she tobogganed down a 5,000+ foot mountain.

Life is always an adventure if you have the right attitude.

Charley never set out to be a storyteller, but looking back on the elaborate lies she made up as a troubled teen she can see that she always had the makings. Now, in the immortal words of Lawrence Block, she happily "makes up lies for fun and profit."

If you would like information regarding Charley's new releases or simply want to contact Charley visit:
    https://charleymarshbooks.com/